I0587148

TAKING KARRE

DIVINITY WARRIORS

MICHELLE M. PILLOW

MICHELLE M. PILLOW® - MICHELLEPILLOW.COM

Taking Karre (Divinity Warriors) © Copyright 2009 - 2018, Michelle M. Pillow

Third Print Edition July 2018

Second Print Edition September 2017

First Print Edition July 2012

Second Electronic Printing April 2012, The Raven Books

First Electronic Printing August 2009

ISBN-13: 978-1-62501-189-3

Published by The Raven Books LLC

ABOUT TAKING KARRE

DIVINITY WARRIORS BOOK FOUR

Alternate Reality Romance

Sir Vidar of Spearhead is too busy guarding the borderlands to bother with the headache of selecting a bride. Ordered to marry by the king, he plans to grab a woman and get back to the warfront, never to think of it again. That is until he meets the alluring Lady Karre with her teasing eyes, lush lips and irresistible ways.

Known by many names, inter-dimensional thief Karre, has only one purpose—take down the company that ruined her life. When her luck runs out and she's caught, Divinity Corporation condemns her to matrimony on a primitive, warrior-filled plane where Karre soon discovers there are worse fates than being prisoner to a man with insatiable appetites.

Before long, days and nights filled with bliss becomes something neither expected, and when Karre is taken, Vidar is forced to confront emotions a battle-hardened warrior never expected to feel.

ABOUT DIVINITY WARRIORS SERIES

In a land forever at war, the Starian men are so busy fighting that their marriage ceremony has been reduced to a "will of the gods" event where they simply pick a woman out of a lineup and claim her as a wife. With women becoming scarce, it's necessary to trade the offworld Divinity Corporation for brides.

They live a very Medieval-like existence. Instead of medical advancement and technology, all of their focus has been on developing weaponry and battle strategy. With places named for war, such as Spearhead and Battlewar, these men have been left in charge way too long. They are in desperate need of a woman's touch.

The Playful Prince
The Bound Prince
The Rogue Prince
The Pirate Prince

Captured by a Dragon-Shifter Series
Determined Prince
Rebellious Prince
Stranded with the Cajun
Hunted by the Dragon
Mischievous Prince
Headstrong Prince

Space Lords Series
His Frost Maiden
His Fire Maiden
His Metal Maiden
His Earth Maiden
His Woodland Maiden

Qurilixen Lords Series

Dragon Prince

Marked Prince

More Coming Soon!

To learn more about the Qurilixen World series of books and to stay up to date on the latest book list visit www.MichellePillow.com

AUTHOR UPDATES

To stay informed about when a new book in the series installments is released, sign up for updates:

michellepillow.com/author-updates

PROLOGUE

Because right now, in this moment, she was their fantasy.

Karre marched out on stage in red stiletto heels, a slinky dress, big grin and nothing else. She kept tempo with the hard, drumming beat of music. Men hollered, whooping their excitement just to see her. She smiled at them, looking over the crowd of heads. She could make them do anything—beg, buy, steal, kill—because right now, in this moment, she was their fantasy.

Blonde hair piled high on her head, garnished

with a string of diamonds and rubies some suitor had given her. It was a sweet trinket, one she might even keep, not that she would remember where the jewels came from. She traveled too much and had more important things on her mind.

Karre turned slowly with her arms raised above her head. The hem of her short dress lifted to just below the curve of her ass. When her back was to the crowd, she bent forward. The cheering grew as the men got a peek of the naked treasure hidden beneath the clinging silver. What did she care if they saw her ass? Her pussy? Her breasts? They were just skin, flesh, a tool like any other. No matter how much they wanted her, they would never be able to touch her.

On this dimensional plane of existence, humans cohabitated with humanoid creatures. The first time Karre saw a vampire sucking on the neck of a shifted werewolf, she'd nearly sprinted out of the room to find her wrist portal to flash out of there to another plane. The portable device looked like a large bracelet to most, but to Karre it was her sole means of survival.

Necessity made her stay where she was. This plane was the easiest to get jewels on without resorting to thievery and the hard, shiny rocks were good for trade in nearly every dimension. Besides, not counting the dancing, being in Dimensional Plane 395 was like taking a vacation. With so many strange and different creatures, they never questioned anything she said and most were focused more on blood-drinking and pleasure-seeking.

Being in a new dimensional plane was like being in your world, but only if had it evolved in a different way. To a point, there were many similarities. Languages, generally, were relatively similar, though for some reason the written word consisted of unfamiliar symbols. Some people looked the same, but were not the same people. Natural disasters and major human events were shared. Weather was the same and each place was still Earth.

"I adore you, Sparkle!" a man yelled. "Marry me!"

Karre turned to look over her shoulder at the crowd and winked. A plethora of large green horns, red flesh, reptile skin, webbed fingers, sharp fangs, and ridged flesh stretched out before her until the mass became a single entity flowing back and forth like a wave.

"I'll take that as a yes," the same voice answered her playful flirting. A rush of similar proposals followed the first, showering her in declarations of love. But she wasn't fool enough to believe them. What they felt wasn't love. It was lust.

Karre knew their adoration for what it was and used it to fuel her dance. She twirled and wiggled, thrust her ass toward them, drew her hips in seductive circles, only to pause in a sexy pose in time with the music. Slowly, she undressed, peeling the slinky gown off her body. Several lights flashed, illuminating her from various angles, leaving no curve unseen.

Just flesh. Just a means. Just another job. Just another plane and soon a distant memory.

Her smile widened, as she knew this was her last dance, at least for this trip. The cheering rose, but she stopped listening. And then it was over. Karre held still, letting the dying notes find their silence before walking naked from the stage.

"You were wonderful tonight, Sparkle," a new dancer fawned. "The crowd loves you. I was wondering if you'd show me how to—"

"Is he here?" Karre asked, stopping the woman from starting a conversation Karre didn't have time for. It's not like she could tell the truth—that all her dancing skill was someone else's memories uploaded into her brain by a device she'd bartered for on another plane.

"He's in your room," the woman answered, frowning slightly at having her question dismissed. "And he brought a large case. I think it's full of gifts so you'll consider his suit."

"Perfect," Karre grinned. Taking a long robe the woman held out, she slipped it over her shoulders. "I don't want to be disturbed."

Two weeks ago, Dimensional Plane 1 5 4, Stac Lesh Mansion
Because right now, in this moment, she was the help.

Karre stared at her red, curly hair in the liquid-silver reflection wall. It had been pulled into a bun at the nape of her neck. The long skirt of the plain uniform and padded body suit did much to hide her figure under the thick gray wool. An apron, changed every time so much as a spot marred the pristine white, covered high over her chest and low to her knees. With the clothes and makeup to pale her face into an unimpressive mask, no one would look twice in her direction because right now, in this moment, she was the help.

She had expected to keep her head down and do her job for months before coming back into this room. But in putting on the uniform, she became invisible. The rich people she worked for didn't look in her direction twice. Well, that wasn't necessarily true. When the wife was gone, the husband had looked at her more than twice. A big grin showcasing blacked-out teeth and a very inappropriately timed belch had changed his interest quickly.

Karre reached to touch her reflection. Behind her, the rich baby's room spread out like the entrance to a palace. Gilded ceilings etched with clouds, golden rays of light and ridiculously cheerful fat angels stretched above as white marble stretched below. It was cold and unwelcoming and more than any one person deserved.

"Oh, wonderful, finally, help," the rich wife said, sweeping into the room. Karre didn't bother to learn the lady's name. "Rich wife" was much easier to remember. The woman held her child under the arms, away from her chest, as if contact with the baby would somehow ruin her carefully planned outfit. "Which one are you?"

"Brigitte, ma'am."

"Take Cinny," the woman ordered. "Mommy needs time to collect herself."

Karre suppressed her groan of frustration at being interrupted and stood to dutifully take the child. She cradled the poor creature close and walked it toward the crib.

"Sing to Cinny before you put her down," rich wife ordered, standing before the liquid silver as she brushed at her clothes.

Karre stopped walking. Sing? To the gurgling, wiggling mass in her arms?

"Well, Brigitte?"

"Mistress, mistress, let me come in," Karre sang the only childlike-sounding song she could think of at the moment, pausing to clear her throat. "I have the pence if you have a quim."

"What a pretty tune," the woman said. "I've never heard it. What does it mean?"

"My dad sang it to my mom," Karre answered, letting the memories she had uploaded into her mind take over her personality—Brigitte of the Fallen Women, a whore's daughter raised in a brothel, adept at blending into new environments. She left off the word "once" before adding the lie, "I'm not sure what it means."

"Carry on."

"Mistress, mistress, I'm stiff as a pin. I need your..." Karre continued, lowering her voice as the woman left her alone with the gurgling, oblivious child. Stopping, she laid the baby down and said, "Sorry, kid, it's the only song I knew the words to. But I guess it's all right. I turned out just fine with lots of jewels and pretty things and you're too little to understand what any of it means. You should be more worried about growing up in this place with that mom of yours. Now, if you just be good," she paused and tucked a blanket around the infant's body, "I've got a job to do."

Going back to the wall, Karre again reached for her reflection. She stepped forward, letting the liquid hit her hand. It stung, freezing cold in the warm room. For a moment, she hesitated, glancing back at the gurgling child. She thought about grabbing Cinny and taking the baby with her.

"Sorry, kid," she whispered, "even with that mother, you're better off here."

It was a delicate balance—keeping her purpose in her mind while living out the personality and quirks of another—almost like having two people in her head. Karre's hand met with the wall as she felt around, searching for the device she'd hidden. When her fingers met with a smooth, flat surface, she frowned. Putting a second hand to the wall she became frantic, sliding her palms in wide, searching arcs. Perhaps the adhesive she used had come loose. She bent her knees, crouching as she searched the bottom corner of the liquid reflecting wall. Her fingers were so cold it became hard to feel, but the molecular structure of the liquid kept the silver from trickling down her arms as it remained bonded to itself.

Then, to her great surprise, warmth gripped her. A hand wrapped her wrist and jerked her forward. She was pulled through the wall, feeling the sting of silver before landing on a hard, stone floor. Gasping and shivering, she looked around the secret room. A wall of computing towers lined one side, next to three technicians silently typing away on their holographic keypads.

"Lose something, Brigitte?" a man asked, coming close.

Karre glanced up from the floor, "No, sir. I have nothing to lose."

"You are extraordinary." The man laughed. Her eyes instantly took in the familiar insignia of the Divinity Corporation. "Finally, we meet."

Karre forced a grin she didn't feel, letting him see her blackened teeth. Knowing what she looked like, she couldn't help but wonder at his choice of words.

Extraordinary? "I wasn't aware we were destined to meet, sir. How lucky for me."

"I can assure you when I'm done with you, you won't feel lucky." The man leaned down, studying her face. He had the militant rigidity of a soldier, from the purposeful jerks of his body to the engraved frown lines around his mouth and eyes. His hard gaze bored into her, filling her with cold dread. She, or rather Brigitte, had seen that look in men's eyes before. They were usually the kind to beat a prostitute the second they couldn't get their pricks hard.

"I've heard that one before," she mumbled, pretending to be unimpressed.

"I'm Director Tomes and..." He paused, lifting the small, wrist-wrapping device she'd been searching the liquid-silver wall for. Divinity had the only known source of top-secret inter-dimensional travel technology and they wouldn't like the fact that someone had stolen it. "I have a feeling you know where I am from. It was very naughty of you to borrow our only portable jump prototype. Our scientists will be very interested in seeing how you got it to work. This device will make traveling to uncharted worlds much easier. No more carting around temporary portals. No more perfectly timed pickups from headquarters. No more rescue parties."

Less supervision so you can do more dark deeds, Karre silently added.

"We'll be able to explore planes at a much faster rate," Tomes continued, as if it was a good thing.

Just like an infectious disease.

"Sorry, I'm not available for science lessons, but if you'd like to make an appointment, I'm sure I can fit you in," Karre hummed in pretend thought, "uh, never."

"Oh, you're going to be fun to break, my dear," Tomes promised. "Talbert. Get her ready to go."

One week ago, Dimensional Plane 25, Divinity Prison Hold
Because right now, in this moment, she was in deep shit.

"Sabina, Frannie, Marget, Sulon, Lo Li, Sparkle, Sunset, Twinkles, Saren, Mariska, Marisa, Ms. Pentafore, Lady Pentafore, Madam Pentafore, Domma Pentafore, Prima Pentaf—ugh." Director Tomes sighed heavily, setting down his electronic clipboard. He leaned over, pressing his face close to hers to look into her eyes.

The dank stone room surrounded her, smelling of stale air and dust and now the distinct odor of Tomes' cologne—gun oil and sweat. Her throat tickled, had tickled for the last several hours, but she couldn't cough, couldn't swallow. Karre didn't move. She couldn't. All she could do was to try to block her thoughts from the director's probing questions. Because right now, in this moment, she was in deep shit.

"I'd be here for hours reading all your aliases. There are twenty-three Pentafores alone," Tomes said quietly. Her eyes stayed fixed on him. Short black hair had been cut tight and neat to his head. Though wrinkles fanned from his eyes, his healthy physique gave him the appearance of youth and power.

Director Tomes had her immobilized. Her arms had been tied, her legs cuffed with chains and a truth box affixed to her head. The device worked by inserting microscopic blades into her brain, causing the sensation of fire to explode into her skull. Internally connected to the machine, she knew exactly which images it pried from her thoughts. She heard and saw everything as it tried to project her secrets into holographic reality for the whole room to see.

In theory, the box would project memories in response to the questions Tomes asked her. It tried to force the truth from the wearer's mouth. In most cases, the device worked. In Karre's case, she had told so many lies, lived so many lives, it couldn't decipher her thoughts from her imagination.

"Why don't you just tell me who you are? End this suffering. We already know your real face, your real eyes, your real hair." Tomes tucked a strand of her brunette hair behind her ear. "You're such a pretty thing, too pretty to be caught up in this mess. Why don't you end this? I'm really not a bad guy when you get to know me."

The last thing Karre wanted was to get to know Director Tomes.

"You know most people have a seizure after having this," he paused meaningfully and tapped the box, painfully jolting her head as he punctuated his words, "on for so long."

Karre forced herself to remember the time she'd roundhouse kicked an attacker in the side of the head. The image played out for Tomes. It was as close to a threat as she could manage without the ability to move or speak.

Tomes stood, sighing heavily. "Fine, don't give us a real name. Don't tell us how you got the prototype to work. It doesn't matter."

Karre repeated the memory.

A tech arrived next to Tomes holding a clipboard and whispered into the director's ear.

Tomes turned a sharpened gaze on her and smiled wryly. "Clever, clever girl. I see you've been to Plane 23. No wonder our truth box doesn't work on you. You do realize you are dangerously close to scrambling your brains each time you implant someone else's stolen memories into your head." He grabbed her face, squeezing it in his palms. "How often do you use it? Do you even remember who you are?"

Karre fought the answer to that question as it tried to crawl out of the darkened corner of her brain. Yes, she used the memory implantation device, but only to help her stay in character when she went undercover. When she changed herself like that, the truth of her goals stayed, but it became buried in the thoughts and speech and look of another's life.

Mistress, mistress, let me come in. I have the pence if you have a quim.

Brigitte's bawdy, childhood song echoed through her mind and she knew the box played it for her captors. The memory of being a child, hidden in the closet while yet another man sang that song shot through her. The technician looked shocked. Tomes chuckled. Karre knew that it wasn't really her childhood, but she felt the deadness of Brigitte inside her.

"Where you're going, you won't need a name or a past," Tomes said. "You'll just be some man's property. Where you are going, we'll always be able to come and get you, but you will never be able to leave. Have fun in Staria, sweetheart. They're going to love a feisty little thing like you and I guarantee they will put you up for a role you've never played."

1

UNDESIGNATED PLANE NUMBER, OUTSIDE BATTLEWAR CASTLE, STARIA

Because right now, in this moment, she was a little cramped for space.

Play dead or fight her way out? As feeling slowly came back to her limbs, Karre tried to discreetly stretch her legs. Her thoughts ran rampant, some her own, some implanted. This part of the process, the coming down from the virtual drug of another person's life, always made her feel a little crazy. She found it best to concentrate on the present during these times. It looked like playing dead was her best option. Running away might be a bit hard, because right now, in this moment, she was a little cramped for space.

Two of Divinity's henchmen dragged her behind them on the ground, carting her in a canvas sack on what felt like a flat board with two small, crooked wheels near her feet. Her body jolted painfully as she bumped over the rutted earth.

Before they left, Karre had watched as Talbert and a couple of others dressed in primitive clothing—long, loose, threadbare tunic shirts over tighter brown pants and boots. Tomes' team of scientists had time to study the prototype she had stolen from them, figuring out how to make it work, while she was busy playing maid.

Sure, I do all the calibrations and they'll claim it as their achievement. Too bad they don't know the little secret about it yet.

Their first unofficial, unsanctioned Divinity Corporation trip had been to take her to this strange, primitive plane—Staria. Out of the four-hundred-thirty-six dimensions on Divinity's corporate-approved chart, she didn't recognize this one as one of them. And Karre had pretty much seen them all and more. Unfortunately, she didn't remember the jump since they'd knocked her unconscious.

She wondered how human this reality was. Karre had seen a lot of things in her travels—crazed worshippers bent on human sacrifice, a tribe of women who only ate bugs, people who danced in circles at every sunrise. She'd even seen men who alternated wives daily, moving from home to home until no one knew who fathered a child. Each generation, the offspring would move to different villages to prevent gene contamination.

Logically, she could assume most of the people in her current plane of reality had never even heard of dimensional travel or portals. Divinity wouldn't want her dead in case they decided later that they needed her—whether it was to get her help with the portal device or to try her for crimes not yet known. And what they didn't know about her activities was quite a lot.

Karre bit her lip. Just to see if it would work, she rocked her body as she hit a hard bump, trying to fall off the makeshift cart. She barely made it a quarter turn before a rope jerked her back into position.

So much for escape.

Watching yet another large horse pass by the small hole she had managed to work into the canvas sack, she frowned. Servants carted water along unpaved roads. The sound of voices mixed with the clomping of hooves and the squeaking of carts.

Natural light and even more natural smells surrounded her. No motors ran, no flying machines squealed, no electrical hums resounded constantly in the background. Staria was as primitive as could be imagined.

Well, that's not exactly true. There was that one plane that had nothing but furry monkey men throwing dung at me. What a mistake in dialing that one was.

Karre snorted at the memory before she could think to stop herself.

"She's awake." She recognized the whine of Talbert's voice.

"She's not going anywhere, not strapped down like that," the other captor answered. She couldn't be sure who he was, but her best guess it was Talbert's leering buddy, Winston. "We're almost there."

"What if she screams?" Talbert inquired.

"Let her. Look around. No one here will care. Why do you think they chose this place?" A boot nudged her hard in the back and low words hissed through the sack. "You hear that, thief? Scream all you want. We have papers here that will land you in Starian prisons for the rest of your life. Behave and you just may be allowed to roam free."

These men didn't know her very well. Karre was

not a scream-for-help kind of girl. She had gotten caught and she would get herself out of it. She didn't need a do-gooder trying to save her. Besides, asking for help only meant you ended up owing someone. She would be beholden to none. Though being allowed to roam free sounded much better than being in a prison.

Karre angled her head, inhaling deeply through the hole. The air was fresher than what she had in the bag and she took several breaths before again looking at her surroundings. The motion of her body stopped as her carriers halted in their progress.

Two legs passed close by her peephole. She heard part of a conversation, said in a man's laughing voice, "...your bride. You should be happy."

When she could again see, it was a full view of a masculine hip. Sunlight hit his crotch, outlining the gentle bulge in his tight black breeches. Instantly, she took in the details. Thick hand-stitching ran along the side of his thigh, ending at his narrow waist in tightly knotted laces. The muscles of his thigh flexed as his weight shifted. A strong hand fell down, revealing a scar over the back of his wrist, only to lift back up.

"Duty demands I be here," a deep, resonate voice answered the first. The sound sent a tiny quiver of chills over her body and she wondered if she was remembering someone else's feelings. "I would much rather the king chose a wife of even temperament for me. Then she could be delivered to Spearhead and I would not have to leave my post. These ceremonies are a waste of valuable time."

"Why would you not seek to choose your own bride?" the laughing voice asked.

"If the—" the deep, sexy voice answered. Karre's body was jolted as the two henchmen began to walk once more.

"Ah," she whispered, curiously trying to listen to and watch the conversation. It was of no use. Her captors quickened their pace. She managed to get a fleeting glimpse of the man's chest, but he turned his back to her and his face remained just out of view.

"I DO NOT KNOW why you look as if someone is forcing you by knifepoint to claim your bride. You should be happy." Sir Oskar laughed, lifting his hand to wave at a merchant selling racks of dried meat near the edge of the marketplace. The merchant pointed at a slab of dark meat. Oskar waved again, holding up five fingers to indicate the quantity of his purchase without actually talking to the seller.

Sir Vidar of Spearhead sighed, absently watching his friend order supplies for Spearhead Fortress. He placed his hands on his hips and glanced at a couple of men carting a pile of canvas on a slab of wood. They had ridden all the way to Battlewar Castle from the southern borderlands and Vidar determined that they might as well make full use of the trip. He gave a rueful smile, not repeating his thoughts out loud. Many of his people might disagree with him that fetching a bride didn't make full use of a trip.

Bright sunlight mixed with a warm breeze. It was a fine day to walk through the market. Permanent booths of the local tradesmen butted against the inner bailey wall, packed tight with merchandise. Off the main road through town, traveling merchants had set up horse-drawn carts side by side, and sold wares out of the back. They decorated them with brightly colored strips of material to draw the eye. The booths were clustered together to form narrow walkways impossible to pass through on horse, which was why Oskar and Vidar had abandoned their mounts within the inner gates to be stabled near Battlewar Castle.

"If I appear cross it is only because I do not like

the wasted time. Alas, duty demands I be here," Vidar answered after a long pause.

He dropped his hands, twisting to watch a woman with flowers dance and sing her way around them. She winked at first Vidar and then Oskar in invitation. Vidar smiled back automatically. Women were scarce in his world. Males became a necessity for battle and their natural evolution seemed to answer the call with more sons than daughters—when they did have children. Their low birthrate wasn't from lack of trying when the warriors were home, but war took them away all too often. Sometimes forever.

By the look of the woman's escorts trailing behind her, she already had at least a couple husbands. If necessity demanded it, he would allow his wife to take another husband, but he would definitely be the first. Sighing, Vidar continued, "I would much rather the king chose a wife of even temperament for me. Then she could be delivered to Spearhead and I would not have to leave my post. These ceremonies are a waste of valuable time."

"Why would you not seek to choose your own bride?" Oskar asked, the humor still thick in his voice. His friend found much amusement in Vidar's orders to find a wife and bring her back to Spearhead

Fortress. Vidar had been one of the six chosen for the ceremony because of his position of power at Spearhead. To see their commander married would give hope to the people of his keep. To see a Starian leader married to the first batch of traded Divinity brides would give all Starians hope in the future.

"If the Caniba attack while we are away, I might miss my chance to discover what Sorceress Magda is up to. We are so close. I can feel it in my bones." He absently watched the cart being pulled away. The canvas moved and he frowned, wondering what it was they carted. He wasn't really worried, just curious. All of Battlewar Castle had been designed for war, just like everything else in their land. If these men didn't belong past Battlewar Town's outer bailey wall, they would never have made it past the heavily guarded front gate.

"I will have the supplies loaded and on the way back to the borderlands before you are done with the breeding ceremony," Oskar assured him. "We can ride out as soon as you claim your woman."

"Good." Vidar nodded. "Send some of the men a half-day's ride from here to put up a tent for my bride. With such a quick departure, I will give her whatever comfort I can while we travel—at least the first night."

"Do you think these otherworld women will understand our ways?" Oskar asked.

"A woman is a woman," Vidar answered indifferently. "The gods will give me what they give me. The king showed me the trade agreement. The women must be able to bear children, be in good health, able to do their duty and will know their place. What do I care if they are born in Staria, or are brought through the fairy rings from distant lands, or are traded for with Divinity aliens from another plane of existence? So long as she is not our enemy..." He shrugged, waving his hand in dismissal of the subject.

Okay, so a part of him wanted a bride, but for purely sexual reasons—someone soft and sweet, someone strong and silent, not too pretty, not too bold, not too needy and not too demanding of his time. He had maids to clean his home, cook his food, sew his clothes, but they were all married and off-limits. What he didn't have was a woman to warm his bed.

Vidar had much to give a wife. He was a strong warrior, a capable provider. He had the skills and means to protect his woman, and he lived close to the battlefront with many opportunities to bring honor to his name. "You order the supplies and pay the coin.

I'm going to the castle to ready myself for the ceremony."

"It is not until tomorrow," Oskar teased. "How much readiness does a man need?"

"Off with you," Vidar grumbled good-naturedly. With that, he left the market and made his way toward the center of the city to a shorter inner wall that encircled the castle, including the exercise yard where the knights trained, a small chapel, and the stables. Several of the soldiers lifted their hands in greeting but didn't stop him. He didn't want to talk to anyone right now. Seeing the two strange men with the cart hauling their sack toward the servants' entrance, he turned in the other direction.

The moment Karre sensed the busy streets were well behind them, she began to squirm inside the sack. She reached for the peephole, tearing it open with a loud rip. She had heard their plan to take her into the servants' entrance of a castle and knew that if she wanted to escape, now would be her chance. Who knew what kinds of horrors awaited her inside this Battlewar Castle? It wasn't like Divinity had to operate under any kind of humanity laws. Her first thought was she was being sold as a sex slave. She never really made it to a second thought.

"Stop her," Talbert yelled to his companion. His red face looked more like a natural condition than the result of the excursion to the castle. Karre bucked up from the cart, ignoring her pained muscles. Like a feral cat, she leapt, striking out with her fingernails. The crashing weight of her body had more effect on him than her hands as he fell back in surprise. Her limbs ached and she didn't get up as fast as she would have liked. Spinning, she found the thick-jowled Winston fumbling with a vial and injector. They'd planned on drugging her again to keep her compliant.

With the cart between them, he could not stop her as she darted into the narrow castle door. Not stopping to consider her route, she ran, turning corner after corner. The long white, shapeless gown covering her body hampered her legs and she jerked the skirt up. At first, she heard the henchmen behind her. It only made her run faster.

It was dumb luck that she managed to run unseen through the maze-like halls. As the sound of pursuit faded, she slowed, trying to get her bearings. Her bare foot stepped on a stone and she gasped, half hopping, half jogging as pain radiated up from her arch. The blue-gray stone walls and minimal decorations made it hard to track where she was going. Wooden doors were spaced evenly on each side with lit torches burning brightly in between.

When the pain didn't lessen, she was finally forced to stop and lean against the wall to check on the injury. The stone had punctured the delicate flesh. Frowning, she realized she had left a blood trail on the cold stone behind her.

Careless. Very Careless. Shit.

Unexpected movement caught her eye and she gasped, dropping her foot. It was too late. A man walked around the corner, crashing into her. Initially, she thought it was one of the guards and made a move to strike. The man grabbed her wrist with lightning fast reflexes, stopping her blow before it even began.

"Hold," he ordered.

Karre blinked in surprise. That voice, a stranger's yet oddly familiar. It was the man she had watched through the peephole. Her breathing deepened and her heart quickened. She wasn't prepared for the reaction and she found herself staring at his broad chest. The smell of him captured her senses. He was earthy, fresh, like the wind through a forest. Heat radiated up her arm from the firm grasp. Her eyes trailed down to that hand, seeing the scar along his wrist. It confirmed what she already knew.

His simple linen over-tunic fell loose to his hips, not covering the pants she had admired earlier. His arms were left bare—thick, muscular arms. A black tattoo wrapped around his upper bicep, the lines bold and confident just like she imagined the man to be.

She bit her lip and pressed her legs tightly together. Firelight danced over his flesh, illuminating every dip, curve and puckered scar. She found her gaze going to the bulge between his thighs—strong thighs surrounded a thickening cock. A woven belt wrapped loosely around his waist, holding a sheathed knife. Her hand flexed and she forcibly stopped herself from taking the belt in hand. Opposite the short blade, his sword hung from a shoulder scabbard that crossed his chest.

"You are dressed as a bride." The statement was simple and matter-of-fact.

Karre blinked, looking up at his face, almost afraid to see the man who went with the voice. Hazel brown eyes met hers. Yellow flecks ringed the iris and spread out like little starbursts in his eyes. Lids lowered in an almost animalistic way.

"I'm dressed as a..." Karre frowned, comprehending the word. "Bride?"

Did he say bride?

"I thought you were to stay in the..."

Blend in, Karre. Do not draw attention to yourself. Be what you need to be.

Karre cut off his words, placing her hand over his scarred wrist as the sound of running feet came from behind. "Please, hide me." The words were purposefully breathy and meek. Big strong men usually liked their women mild-mannered and controllable, so she went with it. She lowered her eyes, letting her lashes fall and her lips tremble. "Please, don't let them hurt me."

The hand on her tightened. The man glanced back and forth down the hall. "Come with me." He ushered her into a nearby room, quietly closing the door behind them.

Karre leaned her ear to the door, unable to help smiling at the sound of two henchmen running past. Pushing away from the wood, she turned. "Thank you."

His narrowed eyes watched her for a moment before turning his attention to the door. "Are you in trouble? Who are those men? Are they—?"

"We should stay here," Karre interrupted. She

took quick inventory of the room. It was a sleeping chamber complete with trunk, small bed and a disturbing amount of weaponry hanging on the wall. "Just for a little bit until they're gone."

"Who are—"

"You were saying something about a bride? You're here to get married, right?" She kept her eyes wide and innocent, all the time taking in every detail of his reaction. Pulling at her waist, she discreetly drew the material so it pulled snug to her chest and hips. The motion had the desired effect. The man's eyes went to her breasts.

"Yea, I am one of the firsts. The king has ordered me to the ceremony to choose a bride." His breathing deepened.

"Choose? You don't know who you will pick?" How peculiar.

"No. I do not." He shook his head in denial as the tip of his tongue appeared along the bottom edge of his mouth. "I do not have an understanding with a woman. I will choose who the gods will me to."

"Who the gods will you to?"

"Yea. I am told that those men who do not have an understanding with a woman are filled with an urge by the gods during the ceremony. In that moment, they know who to choose."

An urge? Is that what they're calling it nowadays?

She tried not to laugh. Karre found herself looking at his mouth with lips so full and firm. She bet he could kiss a woman breathless. How long had it been since she'd been kissed? Two months? Five? Ten? Twenty? Days ran together, blending into months and years. Logic and reason told her now was not the time to fulfill her neglected lust. Now was the time to keep a level head and make good an escape. Now was the time to find a portal out of there.

Logic and reason were very poor defenses against lust.

"So tonight is your last night as a free man?" She licked her lips so they would glisten.

"No, I am not to be imprisoned." He frowned, confused.

Karre did laugh that time. She took a bold step for him. Why not give in to her base desires—if the desires were really hers and not some residual impulse from someone else's implanted emotion. Remembering how Brigitte wasn't really interested in men, she pushed all echoing thoughts from her mind. Tonight was hers, no one else's.

Karre needed to bide her time before going back out into the hall and what better way than with a virile hunk of a man? It wasn't like she would see him again. It wasn't like sex with him would compromise any objective. "I meant your last night free from the bonds of an arranged marriage."

"Then tonight is your last night free as well," he returned. "Your clothing indicates that you are to be a chosen bride."

Karre didn't care what her outfit said. She would be no man's bride. "Perhaps no one will choose me."

He laughed. His entire body shook with the force of it. "No bride has ever gone unchosen."

"Hm." She kept her expression steady, not finding the same humor he did in the idea of her future as a Starian wife. "Then we should not waste our last night of freedom talking."

"You are part of Divinity's trade agreement," he said, as if suddenly understanding her strangeness. "Forgive me, I should have realized since only women from the trade agreement are going to be at this ceremony. That is why you speak so strangely. You are not from Staria."

"Trade agreement?" Interesting. Very interesting. Though hardly surprising. Nothing about the corporation surprised her anymore. With an actual Divinity trade agreement in place there would have to be portal travel to and from this world. Director Tomes might want her to believe she was dumped on a primitive plane to be forgotten, but where there was a portal, there was a way out.

"Yea." He nodded. "You are here in trade for the blue mineral water that runs in our underground springs."

"Am I?" She arched a brow, listening closely. Perhaps a quick romp wouldn't be the only thing she got from his warrior man.

"I am happy to see you do not look pale and weak like the first of your people to arrive. I have heard stories from the men who were there that day when the Divinity aliens first approached us in the midst of battle. We almost slaughtered them where they stood for being allies to the Caniba."

"The Caniba?" She licked her lips again, surprised by his forthcoming conversation.

"Our enemy. They are a dishonorable, disgusting people who eat the flesh of men and think only of pleasing their overlords. The most deadly of which is Sorceress Magda. Her army drinks the poison of snakes and would follow her orders into a pit of fire to be burned alive." His face darkened into a temperate rage and he looked past her.

Karre grimaced. The man surely knew how to kill a seductive mood. Didn't he realize she was flirting with him? "Surely they are not so bad as all that."

"And worse," he swore. His eyes practically sparkled with the passion of his convictions. "There is no peace with the Caniba, only war. It is my self-given task to discover where the sorceress' encampment lies and I will gladly die for that information, for it will be a great victory for my people. I believe I am getting closer. We suspect she is in the Hanging Forest, very near Spearhead Fortress. That is where I live."

"Well," Karre tried to sound cheerful, "good for you. It is always nice to have a purpose to fight for."

Crazy barbarian.

"Thank you, Lady, ah...?"

Karre ignored the prompt for her name and hurriedly said, "So, how did this war of yours start?"

"It has been that way from the beginning of time and will always be so long as they live. That is the role our gods have given us."

Wow, and the foreplay just keeps coming, she thought sarcastically. *Well, I did ask.*

He crossed his arms over his chest, dominating the room with his stance. "Methinks we get on quite well, my lady."

"Yes." She forced a wide smile. "Quite."

"This is good." He smiled, as a tentative, searching expression crossed his features.

Blend in, Karre. Be what he needs to see. That's it. Smile wider. Lower your lashes.

"What is your name, soldier?" Karre broke their eye contact, not liking his probing gaze. He looked at her as if he were trying to read her soul. She had a feeling he'd be very talented at prying secrets out of someone, should he set his mind to it.

"Sir Vidar of Spearhead."

Karre tried not to chuckle. She gravitated toward him, not taking a direct path as she made her way closer to the bed. Her heart beat faster and she felt a little dizzy. Why did he have to look at her like that, like he could peel away all her armor? All her defenses?

She touched the bed. Everything in her told her to run. Karre normally trusted her instincts. They had served her so well in the past.

But his smell was inside her head and his gold-flecked eyes wouldn't stop looking at her as if he could see within her soul. She ran her fingers through her messily upswept hair, pulling a dark strand forward, trying to get some measure of comfort by seeing which character she was playing now. Her fingers bumped the special, hidden hairpin tangled up in the locks, only recognizing it because she knew it was there. Otherwise, it felt like real hair until twisted straight. Not even Tomes had detected it.

It was her hair—long, brunette, wavy. No wig. No dye. No drug-altered state. She touched her face. No fake pustules. No thick foundation makeup. She bumped her fingernail against her front teeth. No blackened smudges. Maybe that was why she felt so exposed and nothing had even happened. The picture she showed him was all her.

"Methinks your pursuers are gone. If you give me their names, I will see they are punished for scaring you. I am sure they saw your clothes and thought to press their suit should you not be chosen at the ceremony by the firsts."

"I don't want to go out quite yet." This might be her closest chance to feel normal, to see what it was like to be with a man as Karre—not James or Linnie or Sparkle or Brigitte. Then again, she could just stop making excuses for wanting Vidar and could do what her body had been urging her to do from the first moment she'd heard his deep, sexy voice.

None of this matters. None of it. Reality is merely a perception. Each plane flows into another until nothing is real. Nothing is permanent. Nothing matters.

Karre had seen many planes, many existences, and only a few things stayed the same. She could only depend on herself. No matter how noble a person appeared, they would ultimately do the selfish thing and nothing ever lasted.

"Did they injure you, my lady?" Vidar reached as if to examine her and stopped mid-motion. He furrowed his brow, doubtful. "Starian men respect women—we do not hurt them. If someone..."

Karre looked up at him and his words trailed off. "Vidar." She let his name roll off her tongue on a purr.

"Y-yea?"

"You sound like a very honorable man." Karre lifted her hand, letting her fingers glide up the center of his chest. He stiffened beneath her touch, his piercing eyes darting down to where they touched. Animalistic fire radiated off him, jumping from his nerves to hers. She swayed toward him. "And you look like a very strong warrior."

Karre bit her lip, pressing her fingers more fully into him. The contours of his chest molded into her palm, unyielding and hard beneath his tunic. His heart beat a steady rhythm, urging hers to join in.

"And this pleases you?"

"Oh, yes, very much." She nodded. "It pleases me very, very much."

If ever there was a sign from the gods, this had to be it—a bride finding him the day before the ceremony, appearing meek, asking him for help so that he might protect her. She was much more beautiful than he would have asked for. In his experience, women...

Vidar tried not to let his thoughtful frown show. Well, in his experience watching other men's experiences, beautiful women were more trouble and more demanding.

As she took a deep breath, he found his eyes moving from the hand on his chest to where her breasts molded the white material. The generous globes would fill his hands to overflowing. His already half-interested cock twitched and he felt all logical thoughts draining with the blood from his brain to fill his member.

Shiny, brunette waves framed her face, showcasing the brown of her eyes and the fullness of her pink lips. Perhaps a bit of beauty was not so bad—if that's what the gods wanted for him. Who was he to question when she looked up at him like that? When she licked her mouth? When she leaned closer, knotting her fingers in his shirt? What else was this encounter if not an inspection of him as a potential husband? Could he blame a woman for campaigning beforehand? For actively searching for a man with honor and a valiant war record? In fact, Vidar respected it greatly. Decisions such as marriage should not be taken lightly. It was important to be assured that your partner was of good stock. That was why men made the final choice, because women sometimes got too emotional—at least according to his late father.

She tugged up on his shirt playfully. "Let me see you, warrior. Let me see how strong you are."

Vidar did not hesitate as he pulled his shirt over his head. His kind had never been shy about sex, but still a little guilt nagged the back of his mind. He was to choose a bride and he didn't know if it would be this woman. Though hardly unheard of, what he was doing right now, in this moment on this day, wasn't encouraged. His stomach tightened and his cock lifted to the point it ached. The woman could belong to another on the morrow.

But not today.

"Mm," she moaned low in her throat, letting her delicately long fingers trail on his chest. "You are a warrior, aren't you? Thick, big," she paused and her fingers skated down to his waistband, haphazardly following battle scars, "solid." Her breathing visibly deepened and she moved around him, as if inspecting him for her own personal army. "I'll bet you know how to move, hmm?"

"Would my lady care to examine my weapon?" Unashamed, he reached for the laces at his hip while kicking out of his short boots. He pushed his breeches from his hips before lifting his feet out of them. Vidar kicked them aside, liking of the feel of air on his flesh as he stood naked for her. She came fully around him, pausing as she looked at his towering cock.

"I see that it's not just the height and breadth of your people that are big, my lord," she said.

"I am sir," he corrected, "not a lord, though I do manage my own manor. It is very prosperous."

"Do you now?" She gave him a secretive smile.

Before he could inquire about it, she took his cock in her hand and stroked. He inhaled sharply. The woman pressed her mouth to his chest, brushing light kisses along the contours of his muscles. Moaning lightly, she licked at his nipples.

"You are so warm," she said, moving up to nip at his collarbone. She tightened her fist on his shaft. "Why don't you lie down on the bed?"

It wasn't a question. Like a knight untried in

battle, he quickly made his way to the bed and flipped onto his back. His eyes devoured her, wondering what she would do next. He'd been with women, but they were always camp followers, respected whores who pleased the soldiers they followed. Unfortunately, their numbers were few and the soldiers many. Often, after they chose a partner for the night, they would get straight to the matter. It seemed it was the men who always wanted to take things slow, to make it last.

She started to crawl toward him, but he stopped her before her second knee hit the bed. "Take off the gown."

The woman brought her foot back down to the floor and grabbed the gown. Slowly, almost teasingly, she pulled it up. Inch by glorious inch, she uncovered her shapely legs. Vidar gripped the fur pelt beneath him on the bed. Next came her thighs, agonizing in their leisurely reveal. Then, finally, the heart of her sex guarded by a strip of soft, dark curls. Vidar began to grab his cock only to stop. He didn't want to come too fast. He wanted her to do it.

Mm, hips, round and soft and unscarred. Her flesh was so smooth and tan, so perfectly shaped. His mouth became dry as he waited to see her generous breasts. Their size was unmistakable under her gown. He wanted to grab them, bury his face in them until he couldn't breathe. He wanted to fuck her pussy while he sucked her nipples. Some of the knights talked of legs or eyes or a woman's fine backside. Vidar had always been partial to great pair of breasts. His grip tightened on the bed.

Oh, the bottom curves. If he could have moved, he'd have surged forward to rip the gown from her body like a madman. Then, finally, the wait was over. She tugged the gown over her head and threw it aside. The motion tousled her hair around her shoulders, but he barely noticed. His eyes were fixed on the large, dark nipples on two very round globes. They were bigger than he'd thought, if that was even possible.

All thoughts left him as she leaned to crawl onto the bed. He watched them bounce and move, mesmerized. "You are...mm."

"I will take that to mean you like what you see, my sir."

"Oh, yea." He didn't correct her misuse of his title. At this moment, she could call him anything she wanted. By all the bloody swords in battle, she could demand of him anything she wanted. The woman straddled his knees, swaying gently as she reached her hands over her head to stretch. He licked his lips, hungry to test the soft texture of the globes in his mouth. "I wish for you to finish me now."

"You do, do you?" She gave him a slow, controlling grin. Raking her nails up his thighs, she stopped when she reached his hips. His cock stood tall and she leaned over him. Opening her mouth as she looked up at him, she stretched her neck long so he could watch as his cock was swallowed in the valley of her breasts. It was the most erotic, most arousing thing he'd ever seen. The soft mounds caressed him gently and his hips jerked. Her weighted hands pressed him down so he couldn't press up.

Vidar's gaze narrowed in on what she was doing. He was completely captivated. His stomach tightened as he rolled forward to reach for her chest. He pushed her breast into his cock, squeezing it as he rubbed the softness to his turgid length. It was unlike anything he'd ever felt—soft like a pussy, but dry and enveloping.

"You're a naughty warrior, aren't you?" she whispered. He began to deny it when she shifted her weight and pressed her arms to make her breasts surround his penis. "Aren't you a bad one? Do you like it when I do this?"

"Yea." He could barely speak. Vidar fell back, too immersed in sensations as she worked her pliable flesh over him. Thrusting up, he fucked her like he'd never fucked anyone else, would never have thought to try.

"Does the bad man warrior need to be punished?" She squeezed him tighter.

"Yea, my lady. Punish me." He didn't know what he was saying, only that he needed her to continue. His balls tightened and he felt like he was close to coming. Suddenly, she pulled off him and he nearly lurched off the bed at the sudden lack of contact. He'd been so close and now his cock throbbed with the need to squirt his seed all over her.

"I agree," she purred like some sort of feral cat. She scratched his hips, avoiding the one piece of him that desperately needed to feel her. "You do need to be punished."

"What is my crime?" he demanded, almost desperate.

"Here it is the night before you're to take a wife and you're in here with me. I'd say that's very bad of you, my sir." She thrust a finger into her mouth, licking it as he watched.

"Please..." He started to reach for her. Something about the way she spoke didn't evoke shame, but a forbidden sense of desire.

"Good, I like it when you beg me." She scratched him harder. He nearly came undone.

"Please, finish me," he instantly begged.

She sucked her finger, thrusting it in and out of her mouth several times.

"Please, lean over once more," he panted. His heart hammered in his chest.

Releasing the finger with a loud *pop*, she leaned over. This time, she licked the mushroomed tip of his penis to taste him. The thought of those full lips around his shaft made him lurch up. He grabbed her head and thrust at the same time, bringing her roughly down on his cock. When he hit the back of her throat, he moaned, only half way inside.

"Suck me like you did your finger," he commanded. Sweat beaded his flesh and he felt as if he ran the whole of Staria.

She began to and he loosened his hold. But the satisfied smile died on his mouth as she knocked his hands aside and pulled off. She artfully avoided his attempt to pull her mouth back down. "Tsk, tsk. Naughty, naughty, eager knight trying to bruise my delicate mouth with his big weapon."

"Woman," he warned, the threatening tone ripping from his throat. He couldn't think, couldn't see beyond the bounce of her chest, the fullness of her lips.

"What are you going to do, my sir? You going to pin me down and fuck me? You going to teach me a lesson? Show me just how naughty you are?"

Before the last word left her mouth, he had her flipping through the air to land on her back. Her breath left her in a big rush of air. He fumbled between her legs, pushing her thighs open to make room for his hips as he angled his cock toward the glistening heat of her pussy.

The second the tip of his cock felt moisture, he shoved forward. She gasped, closing her eyes as he fitted himself deep. He didn't expect her cavern to be so tight on him, clamping him as he stormed her keep. He groaned, rocking very slightly as he felt the hard grip.

"I have never had a woman feel so..." He moved his hips in a small circle. "It is as if you have never been stretched by a man. I find it very pleasurable."

She held on to his neck, kneading the muscles. He continued with his shallow thrusts, enjoying the pleasure of her body. Bracing his weight with one hand, he cupped a breast. Her eyes stayed closed, but she was panting and shivering as he moved.

"Give me your name," he said, captivated by the woman beneath him.

"Karre," she answered with a gasp. Her eyes flew open as she looked at him, but she didn't say more as her climax hit her hard.

Vidar moaned, finally letting his body spill over. He jerked out of her, spilling his seed onto the bed. With an exhausted sigh, he rolled next to her on the small bed. The fur stuck to his hot, sweaty back but he didn't care.

"Lady Karre," he said, smiling. "I will remember that."

2

Because right now, in this moment, she was...Lady Karre?

Karre? Did she actually tell him her name was Karre? What in the idiotic, brain-dead, body-numbing, pleasure-laden hell had she been thinking? Karre?!

Clearly, she had been taken aback by the way he moved his body. Or perhaps it was the way he looked at her, rather her breasts, with liquid heat in his hazel gaze. The gold flecks tried to lure her in with their animalistic charm. There had to be a reason for her lunacy. Because right now, in this moment, she was... Lady Karre?

Shit!

Relax, Karre. No one will ever know it's your real name. They'll think it a lie like all the others. Divinity would never believe you were stupid enough to use a real name on their "prison realm".

Why couldn't I have just said Suzetta? Or Majie?

Shit, shit, shit!

"Tell me of your world, Lady Karre," Vidar said, his voice filled with the leisured, sated drawl of a satisfied man. His finger trailed over her arm. "I'm curious to hear of the other realms. Is yours like this one?"

Shit!

She pushed up off the bed with an energy she didn't feel. Survival instinct gave her the fuel she needed to fake nonchalance. Her first idea had been to control him, to make him want her, desire her. That had worked all too well. Why did she have to go and say her real name? Each time he said it, she felt a little sick to her stomach because his voice was low and delicious and rumbled the syllable just right. That word was more intimate than any other because no one knew it.

"My home world is a plane like any other," she answered, reaching into her hair to ensure the hidden hairpin was still artfully tangled in the locks. She set to work pulling the locks up off her neck to cool off. "You know how it is. Every plane is just the same world with a different conclusion. People pretty much talk the same—sometimes they look the same. Weather is the same."

"But I have heard of some wondrous devices—boxes that talk, fire that does not burn. I've even heard tales of how one plane has these contraptions that heat your food within seconds."

"You don't say." She had stopped listening. Grabbing her gown, she pulled it over her head and made her way hastily for the door. "I think the halls should be clear now. Thanks for entertaining me. It's been, ah, yeah."

"But, wait—" Vidar demanded behind her. She heard him move on the bed. "Where are you going?"

"Ah, now, let's not get all sentimental, warrior man." She pulled the large metal handle. "Have a nice life and a wonderful wedding. May your bride be...yeah."

With that half-hearted wish, she slipped from the room.

"Getting to know the locals, are you?" Winston asked.

Karre turned, ready to fight, only to run face-to-chest into her henchman captor. The man stood a head above her but had the broad, medically enhanced physique any thug would be proud of. He grabbed her arms tightly. Her eyes rounded. How had they found her? As if to answer her, the bottom of her foot throbbed. She glanced at the floor. Spots of dried blood led to where they stood. How could she have been so careless?

She opened her mouth to call for Vidar for help. If anything, he'd provide a distraction so she could get away. Winston grunted. Talbert shoved the needle into her leg. The sharp pain was followed by an almost immediate numbness.

"He-lp," she whispered, the plea hissing from her parted lips as she dropped into blackness.

WHAT EXACTLY JUST HAPPENED? Vidar frowned at the door as he jerked on his clothing. Grabbing his boots, he tucked them under his arm as followed Lady Karre to demand some answers.

The hall was empty and he went to look around the closest turn. She wasn't there. Vidar growled and threw his boot against the passageway wall. It thudded hard before falling to the stone.

You're a naughty warrior, aren't you?

Now, with her disappearance, the once playful words seemed mocking to him. She had demanded he turn over an ounce of control to her and he'd done it—thoughtlessly, eagerly, willingly.

Naughty, naughty, eager knight trying to bruise my delicate mouth with his big weapon.

She had definitely mocked him. Was this a game to her? Or perhaps a test that he had failed?

Here it is the night before you're to take a wife and you're in here with me. I'd say that's very bad of you, my sir.

Did she consider his succumbing to her to signify lack of honor and faithfulness on his part? But what of her? She was to be married and she had seduced him within moments of running into him.

Irritation completely overrode the pleasure he'd experienced with release. When she walked out, her eyes had been distant, calculating, nothing like the seductive woman who'd enticed him to her bed.

Thinking of it, he groaned. He couldn't get her breasts out of his mind—full, soft, wickedly perfect.

Naughty, naughty, eager knight.

"THE FASTER YOU make them come, the less time you must spend in their presence," the servant whispered.

Karre tried not to chuckle. The woman didn't know how true that was. Or did running out on a man after sex count as an example of what the woman was implying?

Sera's white corset top squeezed her healthy waist and thrust up two very generous breasts. Long blue skirts billowed around her legs. She stared at Karre before turning her consideration to the half-dozen other women in the prison cell. The smell of freshly baked bread caught Karre's attention as she took a loaf and bit into it. Director Tomes hadn't been big on the feeding of his prisoner.

"That is all they want—a vessel to find release," Sera continued with her advice. "Do not expect tenderness, but if you don't deny them, if you don't resist, you'll be treated fairly enough. And if you give them sons, you'll be greatly rewarded. Life here is not so bad."

Karre tuned everyone out, eyeing the guards with Sera. They barely seemed to notice her. She really had no interest in life here, or in the other women in her cell, or in providing sons for warrior men. What she did have an interest in was escape. And, as past experience taught her, she would need to get ahold of some valuables to do it.

A loaf of bread was shoved through the bars, close to Karre's head. She blinked, glaring at Sera, as the woman talked over her. "I'm telling you how to best survive this place, please, listen. Spreading your thighs is easy enough a task for a decent life. Don't bring trouble upon yourself. Let them find release. They are not such boars when they get what they want."

One of the guards sniffed in amusement. The sound was so soft that Karre didn't think the others heard it. Apparently, he was well aware of the scam the guys had going in this place. Tell all the women that if they didn't have sex, the men would become overrun with fierce emotions they couldn't control.

Very clever of them in a primitive, completely predictable male kind of way.

Sera finally left, taking the guards with her. Karre reached into her hair, finding the small hairpin in the upswept mess. A few strands pulled from her scalp as she released it. Giving the other women a once-over, she set her half-eaten loaf on the floor and didn't hesitate to kneel beside the bars. She reached through them, turned the hairpin so it became a hard lock pick, closed her eyes, and inserted the end of the hairpin into the lock and began feeling her way around to see how the mechanism worked.

One of the prisoners whimpered and Karre willed her to keep her mouth shut. They'd already been warned about annoying the guards. Someone leaned close and Karre peeked to see the tall, black-haired lady at her side. The woman carried herself well, as if used to fighting. Like Karre, each prisoner slash assumed bride wore the white, shapeless dress with bare feet. Behind the fighter, a redhead picked at the sleeve of her gown like it contained buried treasure within the thick weave.

"Put it up," the black-haired beauty warned under her breath.

Karre thrust the hairpin back into her hair seconds before a burly man in a hard leather jerkin and dark breeches appeared before them. A long, thin scar traced down the side of his cheek, giving him the increasingly familiar battle-worn look all the other men seemed to favor. She forced the image of a naked Vidar out of her mind. She wouldn't be able to concentrate if she allowed fantasies of the knight to penetrate her brain.

Metal diamonds plated the leather, creating a symmetrical pattern over the guard's thick chest. Karre considered kicking him through the bars so he would be knocked unconscious on the blue-gray stone behind him. The pattern made such a nice target, after all. The man crossed his arms over his chest. "The flaxen one and the crying one. They do not carry themselves well. Take them and give them the philter."

"What?" one of the prisoners screamed. "No, wait! I'll be good. I swear I'll be good. Please, don't hurt me. Please, I'll do anything you want. Do you want me to make you come? I will. I swear I will. I'll do you all!" To disprove her point, her body began to shake and she started bawling anew.

"Oh, please." Karre rolled her eyes. Like having sex with a big, handsome man was anything to be afraid of.

Oh no, please stop, Vidar, her thoughts mocked, mimicking the pleading woman's high-pitched voice in her head, *I don't want to have an orgasm.*

The barred door opened and four men filed inside. Karre stepped back, out of their way. Two grabbed the now sobbing woman and dragged her out. A blonde screamed, kicking and fighting as tears streamed down her face.

As soon as the men were gone, Karre went back to work, her face set as she tried to feel around the lock with her hairpin.

"You won't be able to open it," the redhead said, looking up from her preoccupation with her sleeve. "Even if you did, there would be no escape. You'd have to fight through the warriors' hall, out of the guarded castle gates and run three strikes over open prairie until you reach the forest. Should you survive the wild beasts that live there, you'd soon find yourself prisoner to an even more vicious race of creatures —monsters so fierce and depraved they'll make you beg for death. Trust me. With the war going on in this forsaken place, we're in the better of the two sides."

"Who are you that we should trust what you say?" Karre inquired. Just a little bit longer and she would have it. If they would all just shut up and let her concentrate.

"Name's Paige," the redhead answered.

"Lilith," another said.

"What do they want with us?" the black-haired fighter added. "Oh, I'm called Jayne."

"They want us to be their whores," Paige said. "They don't call it that, but that's what they want—a subservient woman to rub their feet and spread her legs. If you don't, they get pissed and the whole lot of them stares at you like you are demon spawn incarnate and blames you for your chosen warrior's bad mood. It's either fuck them and suck them, or you're treated like the bottom rung of Starian society."

"Again, I ask, why should we trust you? We don't know you." Karre didn't need some stranger giving her advice. "You could be a plant sent here to make us behave with horror stories of what's beyond the tree line."

Perhaps the portal out of here is beyond the tree line.

"I don't care if you trust me, but I know what I'm talking about. This isn't my first time in a cage." Paige tilted her head back and sighed. "They'll be coming to get us soon."

"What's your name, locksmith?" Jayne inquired.

Karre had a rule, one she'd learned the hard way. Never give two names when on a plane. All too often, paths would cross and lies would be found out. "Karre."

It sounded strange to say the name out loud.

Lady Karre, I will remember that.

An involuntary chill worked along her spine, settling uncomfortably hot near her pussy. The man did have a sexy voice.

"Well, Karre," Jayne said. "I don't think we have much of a choice. If we all work together, maybe we stand a chance. Now, I don't know how we all got here and at this point I don't think it matters, but I do know I'm not staying to spend the rest of my life as some guy's sex toy."

"I agree." Lilith stood, as if hoping Jayne would have a logical solution they could use. "We need a plan."

"Fine," Karre grumbled, still thinking of Vidar and wondering how she could manage to get him back into her bed for one more go. Seconds wasn't usually her style, but there was something about the big warrior man that sent moisture flooding out of her pussy.

Paige shook her head in denial. "Don't look to me to join your little band. You're only fooling your-selves. I've been to the Hanging Forest. I made it all the way to the Starian borders and I've seen the crea-tures that wait beyond."

"What about a dimension jump?" Lilith asked. "Does anyone know if this place has inter-dimen-sional travel technology?"

Karre stiffened, pausing in her lock picking.

"A what?" Paige furrowed her brow in confusion.

When it became apparent no one knew, Karre answered, "Staria? It's too primitive. They don't have the technology here. I got a glimpse of the castle when they brought me to this cell. Through a door I saw servants cart water from a well in buckets and the drive wasn't paved. No artificial lights or motorized vehicles. Though there were several large horses."

"I've never been here," Jayne contributed, "but I'm inclined to agree from what I've observed. These prisons don't use lasers or shocks."

"Someone's coming." Karre pulled her arms out from between the bars. She thrust her lock-picking tool back into her upswept hair.

A new guard arrived dressed similarly to the other men she had seen. His nose had a crook across the bridge. He frowned. "Only three new ones?"

"It's all they sent us," said the man who'd ordered the other two women away.

"How's it going, Edward?" Paige taunted, her face hardening to hide all emotion. Karre looked at her in surprise. Maybe little red had some spunk after all. "I see the nose is healing nicely."

"Lady Paige," Edward growled, glaring at her as if he wanted to pull the sword from his waist and run her through.

"Open the door, Eddie," Paige ordered. "Let me break it again."

Edward grumbled but didn't answer.

"I thought there were five new." Another of

Edward's fellow barbarians joined them, completely ignoring Paige's comment.

"What's wrong, Brock? Don't I count anymore in your little ledger?" Paige sneered.

"You are not new," Brock stated, frowning at her in disapproval. "Your lord is waiting for you and I do hope his punishment is harsh."

Paige's smirk faltered. Brock grinned victoriously.

"You already have one of these guys?" Karre hissed, grabbing Paige's arm. The woman didn't look at her.

"Two were not suitable. They were taken away," Edward answered. "Too weak."

"Three will have to do." Brock sighed. Karre arched a brow, slightly offended by his downtrodden tone. As the two men walked off, he added, "I'll tell my Sera to make ready."

A long silence filled the cell, broken only when Paige whispered, "Ladies, welcome to Battlewar Castle."

VIDAR PUMPED his hand over his cock, biting his lip. He couldn't help it. Images of Lady Karre danced in his thoughts, driving him mad. He wanted to kiss her. He wanted to strangle her. He wanted to throw her up against a wall and fuck her.

By all the bloody battleaxes in Staria, he just wanted her.

One taste wasn't enough. He leaned against the wall, bracing his weight with one hand as he pleasured himself with the other. His guest chambers were sparse, like most of the rooms in Battlewar, containing a trunk, a table, an adequate bed, a cushioned chair, a lit fireplace and a wall filled with weapons. There was no need for finery. He wouldn't be staying long.

Vidar knew the necessity of the breeding ceremony for their people, but, as the esteemed Lord Sorin often said, "Nothing in the process of prancing women before the warriors, who pick them based on an urge, guarantees a well-made match." He was inclined to agree. If he chose a bride based on an urge, he'd be taking Lady Karre home with him this night.

The longer his kind went without the exhausting pleasure of the bed, the more their moods were said to be altered—or so their women complained. He pumped his calloused hand harder and faster, trying to get rid of that base urge. Every logical part told him claiming Karre would be a mistake. She was beautiful, dangerous, manipulative. The more he lay awake the night before thinking of her, analyzing every second of their time together, the more he knew she wouldn't be the type of mate he sought.

Vidar switched hands, adjusting his weight. After coming three times that morning, his body wasn't finishing as quickly. He planned on ridding himself of all desire so he'd not be swayed by her pretty face.

He felt the end coming and turned, pressing his back into the wall as he went at it with both hands. Vidar cupped his balls, pumping his tight fist harder and faster. Oh, but how her pussy gripped him. And those soft breasts. Moist, sucking lips. So wet. So sweet. So hot.

The muscles in his stomach tightened. "*Agh*," he cried out roughly as he came. Breathing hard, he looked at the bed where the silken garments had been laid out by a maid. Tradition demanded grooms dress in the shiny clothing. Vidar sighed heavily. It was an odd reminder of what was coming—silk where he was used to seeing armor.

Crossing over to a basin of water, he washed his hands and swore he heard Lady Karre's mocking laughter. He hit the water surface hard with the flat of his palm, making it splash over the sides and onto his knee. The trail tickled as it brushed against him, just like her hair had done when she crawled over his thighs.

Vidar braced his hands on the small table before forcibly pushing up. His cock stirred, as if mindlessly searching for Lady Karre to comfort it. With a growl, he grabbed the shaft almost angrily. It looked as if he'd be coming for a fifth time before the ceremony began.

3

Because right now, in this moment, she was getting married.

Marriage. It was never something Karre had considered. Well, she had considered a fake engagement once, but that really didn't count since she would have gotten off the plane before saying her vows. Here, now, standing in the main hall of Battlewar Castle, she realized there was no way out—no matter how often she searched her rope-bound wrists looking for the portable jump prototype—because right now, in this moment, she was getting married.

A crescendo of laughter and cheering resounded

over the hall. The boisterous uproar had been going on for some time, as excitement pumped through the crowd. Women wiggled and pranced in their tight corset tops and billowing skirts, trying to entice the men. Some of the gigantic knights wore lightweight tunics, others leather jerkins like the guards, others light chainmail and pieces of armor, and still others wore no shirt at all. Big metal goblets had been set before them, next to matching pitchers, on the long rows of rectangular tables. Muscles bulged, littered with puckered scars and tattooed designs.

The light came from a large fireplace on the far side of the room. Like most things in this place, it was immense and towering. Woven tapestries lined the walls in strips of material, showcasing coats-of-arms and various symbols. Karre looked around, studying the artifacts, wondering how much they'd be worth in trade.

Not now. Blend in.

Karre turned her attention to the head table, set high above the hall at the end of the room as a place of honor for the bridegrooms. Out of all the ceremonies on all the planes, she had never seen something as simple as the Starian marriage. Already two of the women had been claimed. Karre frowned, trying to remember their names—Jayne and Lilith.

She hadn't really been paying close attention from the moment it became evident they wouldn't be able to help her escape. The women had discussed fighting, but nothing came of it.

An oversized, ill-tempered man they called Lord Sorin pointed at Lilith, stating the single word, "Mine," and, with that, they'd been married. Next, Lord Ronen, Sorin's brother, pointed at Jayne. "Mine." And so, too, was Jayne wed.

In a way, Karre respected it. No pretense, no lies, just a simple point of the finger, a single uttered word and it was done. There were no promises of never-ending love, of happily-ever-after, of enduring whatever.

She looked at Vidar, meeting his guarded gaze. Karre tried to smile at him, but he quickly turned his eyes away. Her smile fell. It wasn't like she wanted to be married to him, she assured herself. Why should she care who chose her? All the men appeared to be well-built and made of muscles. Sir Vidar wasn't so special. He just happened to be the first one of them she'd run into. Besides, it wasn't like she was going to actually honor vows she didn't agree to.

Karre watched him carefully, taking in his every movement while trying to appear as if she wasn't. Vidar looked at her again and she pointedly ignored him. Two could play his game. She glanced at Paige before turning to look over her shoulder at the watching crowd. A grinning redhead in bright green sank beneath a long table filled with knights. By the way her man's head rolled back and his hand slipped under the table, it was clear the woman was indiscreetly sucking the guy's cock. Karre saw a couple of others do the same around the hall. Oddly enough, no one seemed to notice the bold behavior.

When no one spoke to claim Paige or herself, she turned back to the table. Four men remained, presumably one had already chosen Paige. If she wasn't mistaken, it had to be the man who stood first in line by the way he tried too hard not to look directly at the woman. Each bridegroom wore a different-colored long tunic, reaching to the knees, over tight brown breeches. Woven belts were knotted at their waists, the end straps hanging along the right thighs. All were strong, with proud eyes and humorless expressions. The first limped when he walked, but by the way he stared at the other bride, Karre easily assumed he belonged to Paige. Remaining were Sir Vidar, a brown-blond man with a pronounced scar on his cheek, and a bearded knight with irritated eyes.

Blend in, Karre. Right now you are a bride.

If bold behavior was what these men wanted, then that was exactly what she would give them.

"Oh, all right, I'll start," Karre announced, drawing attention to herself. Paige seemed almost relieved. She grinned at the bridegrooms and batted her lashes, doing her best not to look too long at Vidar as she gave the others equal attention. "My name is Karre. I like jewels, riches, power, servants, fine clothes and to be worshiped daily." She paused and arched a challenging brow, "I also like to get my way. Any takers?"

The brown-blond warrior looked horrified by her announcement and recoiled in his seat. He ran his fingers through his short hair before scratching the scar on his cheek.

"Come on, gentlemen, don't be shy," Karre strode before them, feeling very much like an auctioneer selling herself. She carried her bound arms like the situation was an everyday occurrence. "I only bite when I want to."

Sir Vidar cleared his throat and adjusted in his seat. Karre winked at him, unable to help herself as she witnessed his obvious discomfort.

The irritated man snorted and shook his head in denial. Standing, he said, "I have no wish for a bride. Excuse me."

Karre laughed, highly amused by the way he practically ran to get away from her. Perhaps she'd be the first woman in their history to not be claimed. She supposed if no one married her, she would be free to leave. Ignoring the slight ping to her ego, she dropped her arms in front of her. "Here I am in a room full of warriors and not a one of them is man enough to handle me. I must say this sets a personal record."

"I can handle you." Sir Vidar stood. "Mine."

Karre arched a brow in challenge. Inside, she trembled, unsure if it was fear or excitement that took hold of her at his words. "We'll see about that, soldier."

"Rejoice, Sir Vidar has chosen!" a herald announced their match, trying to hide his laugh. Wild calls sounded behind her, encouraging Vidar and teasing her.

Vidar bowed slightly in her direction before walking toward a side entrance near the head table. She followed behind him, her body eager to feel his, even as a sense of foreboding unraveled in her brain. A strange instinct told her to run, to not follow him even though he led to inevitable pleasure and great sex.

I want him too much. I should run.

She swallowed, suddenly nervous at the realization. How could she keep herself detached when she couldn't stop staring at his firm ass beneath the drape of his long tunic? She listened for his low, seductive voice, liking the way it made her stomach tense in instant arousal. The farther they walked from the main hall, the more she began to ache. Cream gathered between her thighs, wetting her pussy in anticipation. Logic didn't stand a chance.

Vidar wasn't sure if he should be happy or angry that Karre's challenge had goaded him to take her as a wife. After finding release five times, he had seriously thought he was up to resisting her. Instead, his cock had gotten hard at the first look of her in her white gown. The fireplace lit her from behind, showcasing shadowed curves—lush, soft, perfect curves. His hands flexed, his heart raced, and he knew he couldn't let any other man have her.

However illogical the decision might be, what was done was done and it could not be changed now. He was a man after all and a man needed a wife. Karre was more beautiful than he'd wanted, but he couldn't deny the terrible ache in his loins and the desperate need he felt to have her again. The rest would come in time. With Starian marriages, it always did. He just had to trust that the gods knew what was best and had given him the urge to choose his bride.

Pushing open the door to his assigned chamber, he knew that his belongings—all but a change of clothes—were already packed and on their way back to Spearhead Fortress along with the rest of the supplies. He waited for her to walk in, wondering at the expression on her face. It didn't match the almost frightened look in her eyes.

Was she scared? Of him?

"Why did you run from me?" he asked, resisting the urge to pull her into his arms. It seemed strange to ask her that, when there were so many things he should think to ask of his new bride. He opened his mouth but stopped himself from adding, *Did I do something wrong? Did I fail your test for me?* The questions would make him seem weak.

"I had some place to be," she answered. How easily she dismissed him with her easy voice and light toss of her hand, as if his question was nothing. Then, giving a wry laugh, she said, "Apparently, I had to get ready for my wedding day."

"You did not wish to be chosen." Vidar tried to understand. Perhaps time would help him translate her moods, but right now they frustrated him beyond all recognizable belief. "But you said...?"

She stepped close to his chest, looking up at him with steady eyes. The nearness cut off his words. "I believe you claimed to be man enough to handle me, my sir."

"Sir," he corrected.

Her mouth tightened at one corner. "I said sir."

"You said, 'my sir'," he said. "It is just sir. Or you may call me husband." Vidar found it difficult to say the last word aloud to her. It seemed too new, too strange.

Her eyes dipped to settle on the middle of his chest and did not lift back up. "Yes, I suppose I could call you that, warrior man."

She didn't call him "husband". Vidar didn't make her.

Sexual tension held tight in his body, but still he hesitated. This wasn't like before. Now she was his bride, his wife, his mate. The moment seemed to call for more intimacy than before, but as she had said, he was a warrior. What did warriors know of intimacy? Should he say something nice to her? A compliment, perhaps? Ladies seemed to like those. "You appear to be very strong."

Her eyes shot back up with a small laugh. He

looked into their brown depths, willing her thoughts to enter his mind, to answer all his unasked and unthought-of questions without his having to ask them. Those accursed eyes kept their secrets well hidden.

"And you appear to be very strong, as well, warrior." She touched the spot on his chest that had held her notice moments before. Running her finger down a direct path to his navel, she added, "And warm." The fingertip rimmed his belly button through the soft tunic before skimming over the thin trail of hair hidden beneath the cloth. "And firm." Her touch danced in such a way as to bring his shirt up inch by slow inch. "And you smell nice, of herbs and fresh air." As if to prove her point, she swayed closer, breathing deeply. Her eyes closed and she licked her lips. Her fingers found naked flesh on his stomach, but instead of trailing back up, she skimmed his waistband searching for his laces. "And I seem to remember your taste being..."

Vidar's breathing deepened. His hands flexed. This was not how he would have envisioned this night to be, with a bride doing the seduction, yet he couldn't bring himself to interfere with her plans. She wanted him. That was a very good start. Perhaps the gods knew what they were doing. They had given him a woman to slake his desires.

Then what was the little nagging feeling in the back of his soul?

She blinked, her lashes dipping slowly over her eyes. He fell under her complete spell. Those lips parted with a breath that hit his neck, soft and warm. She moaned, so light that he wasn't sure he didn't just merely feel it. He took a deep breath, wondering when the suspension of time would be over and they would again move toward each other. The scent of her flesh, a new memory, but a strong one, wafted over him.

Vidar stayed entranced in her gaze as he lifted his hand to touch her arm. Her fingers loosened the ties at his waist. He shifted his weight, lifting his foot to pull off one boot and then the other. As his bare feet hit the floor, he again touched her arm.

"What do I taste like?" he asked.

She hesitated. "There's an ocean on another plane and when I stand on the cliffs, face to the crashing surf, it splashes very lightly on my face to make my lips taste like a gentle salt and sweet air. You skin reminds me of that. But your mouth is a different thing altogether. Your lips taste like..."

Vidar kissed her tenderly. He gripped her arm, drawing her near. Her breasts grazed his chest, a tease of more to come. Karre's fingers stopped working on the laces as they slid around his waist to his back. She held him to her. Tiny jolting sensations raced over his skin where flesh touched flesh, exploding in his lips, radiating over his back and stomach. His cock reached for her, begging for its own aggressive contact, but Vidar held back, enjoying the taste of her mouth.

"Like a man who should be kissed," she whispered, when they parted to share a joined, shaky breath.

A fine haze clouded her eyes. She kept her mouth close to his so that they breathed the same air. Her hand stayed on his back, keeping him to her. Her lashes fluttered violently and she pulled back, as if stunned by her own admission.

This time the words were harder, not as vulnerable. "Like a man who should be kissed everywhere." Aggressively, she pushed at his stomach, forcing him up against a wall. "Take off the shirt."

Vidar pulled at his tunic and tossed it aside.

"Mm, good warrior," she murmured. Karre leaned in to nip at his chest, biting only to lick at the insignificant wound. Hands slid over his chest, palms flat and exploring. Her lips wrapped around a nipple, pursing for a kiss. He shivered and closed his eyes as she trailed warm kisses along the folds of his muscles.

She touched his sides, his chest, his neck and jaw, all the while continuing the exploration with her mouth.

Vidar massaged her back, crushing her white gown in his hands. He maneuvered it up to reveal her legs. "Take off your gown."

Karre laughed. "You're not in charge, warrior." She bit him harder.

"I am—"

She bit him again, harder still. A small gasp escaped him and the pleasure the tiny pain caused. Karre raked her nails over his stomach, causing the muscles of his abdomen to contract.

"You are not in charge here, warrior," she insisted, digging her nails just a little deeper. "I am."

"Yea," he whispered, finding himself mindlessly agreeing with her. "You are."

"Very good, warrior." The pressure of her nails lightened. She pushed back. "Unlace your pants."

He glanced down to where she'd tried to untie his breeches. The knots had been loosened and retightened in her fumbling to get them undone. He smiled, grabbed a single strand and tugged. She watched as the knot pulled apart.

"Turn around," she ordered. He arched a questioning brow but did not deny her. Karre ran her hands down his back like claws. The cold sensation of the uneven stone hit hard against his chest and stomach. She rubbed his back, exploring every inch with her firm caress. Then taking his wrists, she lifted his hands up so they pressed near his head. His forehead pressed forward and he closed his eyes.

Karre pushed the breeches down on his hips, letting them hang low. She scratched his ass, fondling it with hard, deep presses of her hands. Her tongue ran up his spine. His hips flexed forward, bumping his covered cock into the unforgiving stone.

"Ah," he gasped, his hands dropping somewhat at the involuntary movement. She pushed at his elbows, forcing them back to their original position.

"So many scars." She traced haphazard patterns over his back where he'd been struck with weapons in battle. "Move your arms again and I'll give you another one."

He clenched his teeth.

"Say you understand," she ordered.

"Yea," he panted.

"Good, warrior." She rewarded his obedience with another deep caress, this time along his hips. Her fingers curled around the hipbone, nearing the impossibly hard heat of his cock. Pushing his pants down around his ankles, she said, "Don't move. I wish to look at you."

Rustling sounded behind him and he wondered what she was doing. His breathing deepened and he was sure he'd not be able to take her game. Every nerve tingled with anticipation, as if wondering where and how she would touch him again.

"Kick off the pants."

He did.

"Spread your legs."

Again he obeyed, placing his feet shoulder-width apart.

Her touch came, causing him to tense as it ran as a single finger up his inner thigh to the underside of his ass cheek. Warmth replaced her finger as she kissed him. He gasped, realizing she knelt behind him. A woman had never touched him there, like that, taking so much control. No woman had ever wanted to, not that he knew.

Every part of him focused on her, the whisper of her breath, the bite of her teeth, the lick of her tongue, the bold caress of her fingers as they moved ever closer to his cock. Unable to help it, he angled his hips in her direction.

The unmistakably soft globes of her breasts pressed into his ass. Taut nipples drew a path up as she stood, keeping her body to his. Her hand moved around, cupping his balls. Vidar groaned, leaning his head back. Another hand snaked around to grab his cock. She rocked against his ass, forcing his hips to move, forcing his cock to slide in her fisted hand.

"I've never been taken like this," he said, panting. He balled his hands into tight fists.

"I like watching you move, muscles beneath flesh." She bit his back hard. "Contracting and releasing." She licked the wound. "Lower your hands to mine. Show me how you will move for me."

He hesitated at the command. "You wish for me to..."

"Yes. I wish for you to..." She drew her hands away, placing them on either side of his shoulders as she kept her body to his.

His cock ached even worse now that the pressure of her hand was gone. He pushed back from the wall, not turning as he grabbed himself. She continued to rock along his body, keeping him moving. Slowly, she pulled away. He couldn't hear her feet but he knew from the sudden abandonment of her heat that she had put distance between them.

"Mm, yes, keep going," she ordered. "Show me how well you move, warrior."

The bed behind him made a small creak. He glanced back. She crawled onto the bed completely naked. With her lush ass to him, she didn't see that he watched. Karre maneuvered onto her back and he glanced back to the uneven stone of the wall. But he had to peek again, had to see. She had lain down and parted her thighs. Her hand touched her mound as she rocked against it. A finger slipped into the wet folds of her sex only to come out glistening. Her eyes lifted, meeting his. Her free hand moved up her stomach to her breast to tease the hard nipple.

He pumped his hips harder, so close to coming, so aroused by the very presence of her. His face tightened and he bit his lip. So close. So close. So...

"Don't finish," she ordered. "If you do, I won't fuck you."

A terrible physical pain racked his stomach at the very thought, but his desire to claim her forced him to obey. A little bit of his seed managed to escape on a tremor but he tensed, forcing it not to happen completely. He swiped the tip to remove the evidence and wiped his hand on the stone wall before turning to face her. "Your warrior is ready, my lady."

Karre knew she had to take control of their affair from the start or else she would be forever at a disadvantage. What she didn't expect was to enjoy the game so thoroughly or to be able to bend him to her sexual will so completely. As he stood, so near completion, cock so full that veins ran up the sides to the flushed tip, she took a deep, steadying breath. Oh, but he'd been gorgeous to watch—firm ass, tight hips, rippling back.

She tried to pull her hand off her pussy, but neither her hips nor her fingers would stop what they were doing. Without waiting to be commanded, he came to her. Karre knew she should demand he stop but consoled herself with the knowledge that she had beckoned him with her eyes, thus not ruining her game.

"Fuck me," she ordered belatedly. He was already crawling onto the bed to do just that. He smiled, a small curling twist of his lips that said he noticed the lateness of her command as well. His eyes narrowed, as if to say he intended to do just that.

He came between her legs, not stopping his crawl until the head of his cock was at her slick entrance. With a perfect thrust of his hips, he filled her with his thick length. She gasped at the size of him, even as she'd been expecting it.

No testing thrust. No time to adjust. Vidar pulled back only to strike. Keeping his hands on the mattress, he stayed above her, riding her hard and deep. A low, pained growl escaped him as she grabbed onto his shoulders.

It felt so good, being pounded by the thick warrior and his amazing weapon. Her breasts bounced, drawing his eyes, and he fucked harder. Sweat spread over his face and she realized he was holding back his release, waiting for her to come with him.

He leaned back, drawing her body up so that she sat somewhat on his bended knees as he continued to thrust. She braced back on her hands. Vidar took hold of her hips. The new position pressed his cock tight to the sweet spot of her sex and she jerked in warning of what was coming.

"Ah," Karre cried, tensing so hard she couldn't control herself.

"That's it, my lady," he urged. "Finish for your warrior. Give me my prize."

The intimate words more than anything forced her to come as he wanted her to. She gripped the coverlet beneath her. Ripple after pleasure-laced ripple coursed over her. Vidar grunted, suddenly stopping with a victorious yell of his own. He came inside her, their bodies pressed tight as he trembled and released.

Seconds later, he dropped her hips and fell

forward, nearly crushing her with his weight before he rolled next to her on the bed. Minutes more and the heavy breathing slowly subsided. Neither one of them moved to separate their tangled limbs. Karre was sure she might never move again.

"I believe I will enjoy having you often, Lady Karre," he said, slipping a hand up to rest on her exposed breast. "Yea, oft indeed."

Karre wondered why the bold promise both exhilarated and frightened her.

"Mm, we should get dressed. We ride out tonight toward home. The knights will be waiting for us to catch up to the supply carts."

"Tonight?" She could barely move, let alone ride. She had seen the big horses and knew exactly what he meant. "But I thought we would sleep here tonight. Do we really need to run off so soon?"

"If it is another go at my cock you are after, I'll gladly make sure we find the time." He licked at her cheek playfully, stroking close to her ear. Slapping her ass cheek, he ordered, "Now, come."

She suppressed a groan. So much for controlling him.

Karre would just have to try harder.

4

Because right now, in this moment, she needed to stop staring at his finely tuned ass and figure out her next move.

Karre could take many things with a fake smile, a pretty pout or a well-played blink of her lashes. Riding a galloping animal that bounced her into Vidar's back as she was forced to hold onto him wasn't one of them. If her nerves weren't stinging with wicked purpose, her backside was being spanked by the constant movement until, even several minutes after she had gotten off the horse, her ass was numb.

Glad to have an excuse to walk around, she

heeded Vidar's warning not to wander too far from the makeshift campground. It wasn't as if she had anywhere to go. A fire burned in a small forest clearing, attended to by a handful of knights. The orange, flickering glow danced seductively along Vidar's back as he stood, arms crossed, talking to a new rider who'd just joined them. He shifted his weight, instantly bringing to mind the way she had ordered him to turn his back to her. What in the stars was she doing? Because right now, in this moment, she needed to stop staring at his finely tuned ass and figure out her next move.

Oh, but his ass was so nice to watch. He shifted again and she forced her eyes away. Noticing that several of the men around the fire studied her, she gave them a smile she didn't feel and made her way toward the tree line for a closer look into the depths of the forest.

All traces of Brigitte had faded from the forefront of her mind until the memories felt more like a book she'd read long ago. She knew the story, but the vivid details and feelings it evoked were gone. The mild headache and state of confusion she was left with would pass soon as well. Tomes had no idea how right he was when he mentioned the brain scramble. The implantation device was useful and made staying in character easier, but she wasn't sure how many more times she would be able to use it.

Looking at the campfire, she thought, *Not that I'll have reason to use it here.*

The full moon shone bright over the clearing, illuminating that which wasn't orange with firelight. Beyond, though, inside the denser trees, only speckles managed to pass through to move softly over the forest floor. A stout breeze whipped her hair into her face and she tugged it back, absently pulling the long strands onto the back of her head to pin them into place.

"Your friend, Lady Jayne, has run away from her husband." The low resonance of Vidar's tone warmed her and she turned to look at him. A few of the men moved from around the fire to mount their horses and join the rider who'd come to the camp. "I fear it is not a good omen, considering Lady Paige also ran from her mate."

"She's not my friend," Karre said distractedly, all the while thinking, *Good for you, Jayne. I didn't think any of you would have the guts to resist them.*

And the truth was, Karre hadn't believed it. She'd really thought the other brides were all talk.

"Where are they going?" She nodded to the

departing men. The sounds of hooves beat over the night.

"To help Lord Ronen search. I can spare Sir Oskar and the others for a few days. We are away from the battlefront and no Caniba will harm us during this part of the journey." He glanced around the encampment. Motioning to a low tent, he said, "If you would like to get out of the wind, we could—"

"Wait," she broke in, "do you mean to imply that the Caniba might attack when we get to Spearhead?"

"Yea, it is possible." He nodded. The strange combination of distant firelight silhouetted him while the moonlight contrasted his face into a ghostly pool of irregular shadows. "The borderlands are not as tamed as Battlewar Castle, but I will protect you. It is my duty."

Karre brushed his comment aside. She could take care of herself. Then, as a cold chill crept over her, she shivered. Why hadn't she considered his home before? "What manner of people are the Caniba again?"

"I do not wish to speak of such things to you," he answered. "Not on this night."

Even as he said it, his words from the day before unfurled in her head.

They are a dishonorable, disgusting people who

eat the flesh of men and think only of pleasing their overlords.

"I would have you speak of such things to me," she countered. "If I'm going to be put into danger, I have a right to know what it is I'm facing. Are they really as bad as you said before? Or is the whole man-eating thing just a story to scare tourists?"

"Tourists?" A heavy sigh left him and he instantly dismissed the question. "You have nothing to fear from the Caniba. You will not be running like the others and I will protect you."

He seemed so sure of the fact. Not really lying, she agreed, "No, I have no plans to run away from you." It was true. At this moment, she had no real plans of running away. Her plans consisted of finding something of value she could trade so that she might *possibly* later run away.

"Good. I do not know how much or how little Divinity told you about our world, but you other-worlders do not know this land or the dangers in it." He looked as if he would lift his hand to beckon her to him, but she subtly shifted, letting the heavier shadows of nearby trees fall across her face. She hoped it hid her expressions.

"Do we need to look for Jayne?" Karre asked. She tried to never get emotionally invested with people from the planes she visited, but she couldn't see leaving someone to die a horrible death by cannibals.

"I have promised to keep an eye out for the missing bride, but it looks as though she's gone in a different direction. I need to get these supplies back to the fortress. There are matters there that await me."

"What matters?" She curled her toes in the over-sized boots she wore.

"They are matters of war," he dismissed, as if that answer should have sufficed.

"Are you going to try to find where that Maggie's encampment is?"

"Sorceress Magda."

"Are you going to try to find where Sorceress Magda's encampment is?" She crossed her arms over her chest, not liking the way he spoke to her—as if she were some silly woman who couldn't possibly understand.

"There is no need to discuss it."

"I want to discuss it," she insisted in frustration.

This time the denial was firm, flat, final. Vidar crossed the distance to join her in the deep shadows. "I do not think you should worry yourself with—"

"Then I don't think you should worry yourself with ever sleeping with me again. If you are going to treat me like a child, I'll act like one. This is me pouting." She dodged his hand, not bothering to uncross her arms as she skirted past him toward the fire.

Vidar watched her leave, frowning after her in confusion. He'd been told women had strange moods, but this was unexpected. Women were to be protected. Why would she wish to hear of the atrocities of the Caniba tonight, their wedding night? Surely, Divinity had told her everything she was required to know.

Perhaps this is another test?

The firelight outlined her as it had in Battlewar's main hall, showing the shadow of her figure beneath her gown. His body stirred. She had less brains than a tree stump if she thought of never coming to his bed again. Then, hearing the laughter of the knights as she approached, he tensed. They couldn't see what he did from their position, because the flames would cast her in orange light, but that didn't stop him from stalking after her.

"My lady, please, join us by—" Lother, one of his warriors, said. The man shared a wife with three others and never showed a moment's regret in the decision. Though the man was married and would not seek another, Vidar didn't like the way Lother smiled at Lady Karre.

Vidar grabbed her arm tightly from behind and jerked her with him toward his tent. She gasped, her eyes widening as she looked at him in surprise. He thrust her in front of him and shielded her body from the view of the others. Sudden silence turned to a burst of noise as the men laughed at his supposed eagerness.

After several paces, he pushed open the front flap, pausing so she could lower her head and duck inside. Once they were alone, she ripped her arm from him. At first he couldn't see her expression, but as his eyes adjusted to the dim light, he found her glaring angrily in his direction.

"Lay a rough hand on me again and I will bite it off." The words came from behind her gritted teeth, as if she didn't trust herself not to make good on the threat.

The venom in her words surprised him.

"You had better say you understand or Lady Jayne will not be the only woman running tonight."

Surprise turned into a scowl. He stepped menacingly forward to tower over her. "I do not know where you come from, but in Staria we do not make threats we cannot carry out."

"Do not presume to know me or what I am capable of. Oh, I assure you, the threats I speak out loud are the ones you should be least worried about." A new passion came to her eyes. He knew he'd just met her and he shouldn't be surprised by any of her expressions, but this one concerned him. First meek, almost innocently sweet, then giving, then calculatingly cold, then an outspoken bride, challenging him, controlling him, softly agreeing to stay with him only to now threaten abandonment and much worse. Who was this woman? Which of the temperaments was truly hers? Or were they all her, a mingling of mixed messages and teeming emotions inside one person, changing her as constantly as waves changed the ocean surface?

Then a thought unfurled in his brain, one he could not stop once it started. Lord Sorin had chosen his second wife this night, but the first, Lady Bianka, had tried to play Sorin false, throwing herself at every man who'd look at her. She had burned down Sorin's family home of Firewall before seeking her carnal pleasures at the hands of the Caniba. Those monstrous beasts took what Bianka offered before ultimately taking her life. The tale was whispered amongst the people—a warning to young girls of the price of dishonor, a warning to men of the price of defying the gods.

"Perhaps you did not understand when your place in our world was explained to you." He craned his neck, purposefully trying to scare her. "I will explain again. Marriages are unions, unbreakable, ending only in death. Women are to be protected and cared for. You will not run from me for I will do my duty and protect you, even if I must protect you from yourself. Women are to be provided for. I will provide for you. I will be a generous husband and you will not want for anything that is in my power to give you, so long as you do your duty. Threaten me again and I will punish you. Run from me and I will come for you. You are mine, my lady, and I do not let go of what is mine."

He'd expected feminine outrage at his words, some kind of feverish denial. Instead, her face calmed and her eyes deadened of their angry passions. Vidar did not like the change in her. He did not like the anger, but this coldness was much worse.

So be it, he resigned himself. *I cannot take back my words for I did not lie to her.*

"Death, you say?" She arched a brow and leaned back to study his face. She touched where he'd grabbed her and began to rub. The motion was brief, as if she caught herself and changed her mind. His hand flexed with the urge to reach out and check to see if he had hurt her. He did not think his hold too firm, but then again, he was used to ordering about knights, not women. "So there is a way out."

"I'll pretend you meant to humor me with your wit."

"Anything I want, huh?" Her eyes lit at the prospect. "What exactly is my duty? Because the only explanation I received was from the maid, Sera, insisting I sleep with you in order calm your bad temper."

"Divinity—" he began.

"Knocked me unconscious and dragged me here as a prisoner. That is what I was doing in the hall," she broke in. "I was escaping my captors."

"Prisoner? What have you done?"

"I don't suppose you would believe that I am innocent?" Karre chuckled. She didn't meet his gaze as she began to walk around the tent. The one-room enclosure had been put up in a hurry as the men made camp. Usually, they would only bother with a tent if there was to be rain, instead choosing to sleep outside by the fire. However, considering the quickness of their departure on Vidar's wedding night, he'd ordered the small comfort for his wife. All right, he'd ordered it for himself as well—for the privacy it would afford him with his bride. How was he to know she would fulfill his desires before leaving Battlewar?

He licked his lips, remembering just how good she'd felt. The tight grip of her quivering sex as she came, flooding him with her cream. A low groan sounded in the back of his throat and he fought to suppress it, remembering the feel of her breasts, the look of her parted thighs—thighs that welcomed him to slip inside.

Her feet absently kicked at the fur pelt on the ground, flipping it over before smoothing it right again with the tip of her toe. The words low, distant, she said, "I did nothing wrong."

"Then the gods must have their reasons. They brought you to me. That is the only explanation. I regret that you did not travel here under the greatest of comfort, but if this is your destiny, then there was no stopping your arrival. This is our joined fate."

She gave a soft laugh. "Will you tell me your expectations of my duties, or will you make me guess? Or is giving you untold pleasures in bed to be my only role?"

His cock jerked, completely satisfied with those terms. His head forced him to speak. "Women tend to a man's home, though at Spearhead you will have to merely direct the servants to see to our needs."

"All of our needs?" She gave him a playful smile. "Do you use the servants to—?"

"No, not those needs." Vidar's gut tightened at the thought of any other in her bed. After he'd met her, the idea of his bride taking more than one husband left him feeling a little cold. He did not want to share her talents with other men. The possessiveness took him by surprise. "The gods smile at Starian unions and, once we marry, we do not seek another. We stay faithful because the gods demand discipline. War demands discipline."

"Marriage and war." She laughed harder, though the sound was barely audible. Her shoulders shook. "That sounds about right."

"Sera was correct in her advice to you." His words lowered into a husky murmur. "If you please your husband, he will be of better temperament."

"Out of all the planes, I have never heard that line used in such a way before. Though several times I have been told the penis will implode or explode if it is not massaged. Sorry, warrior, but you're going to have to come up with a better line than that."

He grimaced. "It is not a line. It is true."

"If you insist." She turned fully to him, giving up

on kicking the furs. "So sex and housekeeping in exchange for anything I want? It sounds like being a kept woman."

"Yea, I will keep you." He nodded in agreement. "It is the will of the gods."

Karre tried not laugh, as he misunderstood her meaning. But truly, what he proposed sounded more like a mistress than a wife—at least according to many of the planes she had been on.

When he had grabbed her arm in his bruising grip, dragging her like some piece of chattel into his tent, she'd snapped. The cool resolve of her façade had disappeared. Her arm ached, but she couldn't be sure if it was the memory or an actual pain that stung the nerves.

Foolish, foolish, Karre, she admonished. *No game is won without thinking, without control. Take back the control.*

Funny how, in all her travels, she had never been put in this position. Sure, she'd had the chance to be a mistress. The course of action would even have been easier than, say, becoming the maid with blackened teeth and frizzy hair, but she always felt she was above using sex to get what she wanted. Okay, so as Sparkle, she had used her sex appeal, but it was hardly the same thing. A pang of guilt wrapped around her heart. That was exactly the arrangement she was making now. At least she was attracted to Vidar. He would make a fine lover.

Yes, lover, not keeper. That is how she would think of him. Lovers gave gifts to their mistresses all the time. It was not the same thing as stealing from him.

It's all about perception.

"You do not speak of love," she observed, "only of protection and sex."

"Unions are made of necessity, not love," he said.

"I'm glad to hear it. I would not have believed you if you said you loved me." Karre ignored the small ache the admission caused, refusing to give the tightening inside her chest any credence.

"Starians love their country, their people, the sanctity of life, but there is no room for romantic love in our world."

She coughed, pressing against the center of her chest. The knot didn't loosen. At his concerned look, she explained, "Dust from the ride. I'm fine."

"Would you like me to get you a drink?"

"Yes, please." She nodded. He disappeared out of the tent.

Get control, Karre. Keep it together.

Karre absently pulled the clips from her hair, fluffing the locks in an effort to enhance her appearance. She looked down at the shapeless gown and frowned. With nothing else to replace it with, she pulled the material over her head and tossed it aside. Then, lying on the fur, she positioned her body carefully, tugging a wayward strand over her shoulder to curl around her breast.

"My lady, your—"

"Ah!" Karre gasped, covering her chest as a young knight walked in with a goblet. He made a strange noise, dropping it on the dirt floor. Red liquor flew across the tent making a slash over her stomach. "Watch it!"

It all happened in an instant. The young man stood, gaping at her waist where the liquor stained her flesh. She tried to push up, but with her arms over her chest, she wobbled and had to brace herself. The gesture exposed a breast. The man made a strange strangling sound before running from the tent as if the fires of hell were after him. Karre let out a burst of laughter.

"I brought food," Vidar said as his hand appeared inside the flap. "What did you do to Groff? He ran into the forest looking like—" Vidar skidded to a stop, looking at her on the fur. He began to smile, but the look faded as he glanced behind him, back to her naked form, behind him once more. "I will string that boy up by his toes."

"Wait." Karre pushed up to stop him. "Leave him be. I think the fear of what you might do was enough. It's not like he knew what he was walking into." When he looked as if he might protest, she hurried to add, "What have you brought me?"

"Oh." He looked at the trencher he carried. "Meat. The men roasted it on the fire."

Karre lay back down, letting her fingers dance along the fur, as she purposefully drew attention to her naked waist. "Bring it to me."

"Did Groff...?"

"Did he look?" Karre laughed, stretching along the fur. "A naked woman was lying on the floor in an otherwise sparsely decorated tent. Yes, he looked and then he ran for his life. Let him be."

Vidar's foot hit the goblet as he stepped forward. It spun and skidded to the edge of the tent. Karre leaned upon her elbow, cradling her head in her hand.

"You're not scared of me, are you, warrior? You won't run away to the forest, will you?" She turned, angling her shoulder back as he neared, giving him free view of her chest.

He knelt, shaking his head in denial as he set the plate near her chest. Karre reached forward to run the back of her hand against his cock, massaging him through his clothing. Already he was eager and hard. Vidar groaned.

"That knight got me wet," she said. His groan turned into a scowl of rage, until she pointed at her hip. "He spilled wine." She trailed a finger along her waist where the liquor was beginning to dry and stick.

Vidar moaned softly. Warm lips brushed her flesh and he began to lick her clean, sucking and biting at her flesh. She kept her hand on his cock, light and teasing. He slid his hand over her ass, cupping her cheek. When he slid his fingers along the back of her thigh, inching them to enter her pussy from behind, she stopped him.

"I'm hungry, warrior. I wish for you to feed me." Karre knew she had her practical reasons for wanting to control him, but as her plan formed in her head, she found she liked their game. If she let him explore her as he'd been intent on doing, she wouldn't be able to keep a straight head.

Vidar lifted a piece of meat from the trencher. Karre pursed her lips and shook her head, refusing to take it. She rubbed his cock harder, rolling forward just enough to reach his balls.

"Take off your clothes so that I may feast." She licked her lips.

Instantly, the shirt was pulled off his chest and thrown at the side of the tent. In his eagerness, he shook as he jerked at the laces. Standing, he kicked his feet to rid himself of his boots as he pushed off the pants. Karre put her head on her hand again, resting against it.

"Feed me," she ordered, not moving as she opened her mouth wide.

Vidar grabbed his cock, stroking it a few times as he knelt back down. The towering shaft bobbed near her face. She reached out with her tongue, licking the smooth tip. He touched her breast, lifting it in his palm, smashing the nipple with his palm until it hardened against him. Walking forward on his knees, he brought his erection closer. Karre sucked him a little deeper, taking the full head into her mouth. Her lips hooked on the ridge as she sucked.

He groaned, reaching over her head. Vidar crawled on top of her, straddling her shoulders as he rested on all fours. The motion turned her onto her back and angled his cock toward her face. Karre gasped in surprise and he took advantage, thrusting his cock deeper into her mouth, nearly choking her on its thick length.

She took hold of his hips to control the depth. His hips worked, fucking her mouth, gliding along her lips and teeth. When he learned the limits of her mouth, she took hold of his balls, rolling them as she sucked hard.

"I enjoy feeding you," he whispered, the admission harsh as it came from above her head. Karre's lungs burned and she was forced to push his hips, taking his cock from her mouth. Protesting, he groaned. "I am not finished. I wish for you to drink me as well."

Gasping for breath, she pushed her large breasts together and looked up at him. His eyes glinted as he got her meaning. All thoughts of her sucking him to completion must have left him because he hungrily lowered his body along hers until his cock fit in the crease of her breasts.

"Now you may come," she said, as if granting him permission.

"Oh," he grunted, pumping so his inner thighs pinned her body down. The intimate smell of his erection filled her senses as the wide tip bumped into her chin. "I enjoy your breasts. So warm and soft and full." He began to find release, the movement of his hips becoming jerky. As he came, he kept moving, spilling his seed over her throat to form a warm necklace before drawing the moisture between her tightly pressed breasts to make his cock slide in his own juices.

He stopped, breathing hard and not moving to take his cock from between her breasts, even as she released their hold on him. Karre raked her nails up his hips and moaned. He might have come, but her body's arousal was merely heightened by the display.

He crawled down, staying above her as he kept her against the floor with the canopy of his body. Bending at the elbows, he leaned down to kiss her mouth.

"I am wet again, warrior," she said before his lips could find their mark.

He furrowed his brow as he looked at the cum he'd squirted around her neck. She saw the moment realization dawned on him. Karre laughed as he reached for a discarded piece of clothing to wipe her clean. The rough material scratched her skin. When he finished, he grinned as if he thought himself very clever. He leaned to kiss her again.

"It is your turn to dine," she said, stopping his mouth once more. She pushed at his shoulder and spread her legs until they bumped the barrier of his body. When he didn't move fast enough, she slipped her hand between them and began rubbing her clit in tiny circles. "Fuck me with your tongue."

He followed her gaze down to where she masturbated. "You wish for me...? I have never dined on a woman there."

As if fascinated and hesitant at the same time, he crawled down her body. She threaded her legs along the outside of his. He licked his lips and she nearly screamed at the seductive agony of his contemplation. Slipping two fingers along the folds, she parted the soft lips. Then, reaching for his hair, she pulled him to her pussy before falling back onto the furs.

Hot breath fanned the parted folds and she pushed on her heels to lift her ass off the ground. His tongue reached slowly to her clit to flick the bud, as if tasting a foreign dish for the first time. He drew his tongue back, as if sampling her intimate taste. A low moan escaped him as he did it again. Then, with increasing eagerness, he ran the flat of his tongue up her folds, over her fingers.

Vidar adjusted his weight to lie more comfortably between her legs. He grabbed her wrist and tossed her hand out of his way. Like a starving man at a fresh spring, he began sucking and drinking her pussy. His hands grabbed hold of her legs, keeping her firm to his mouth as he smothered his face into her folds. His nose stroked her clit as he shoved his tongue inside her cavern. He moaned, vibrating her with the sound. Never had she had such an enthusiastic partner.

Karre bit her lip as she came against his face, shaking and trembling as her moisture coated him. He didn't stop and the sensations became too much. She pushed at his head, gasping, "Enough, Vidar, enough."

He pulled back with a self-satisfied grin. "I will be doing that again, my lady, but for now your taste has made me hard." He crawled up her body and she felt the heat of his cock brush her thigh. The velvety smooth shaft was heavy with desire. "I would like to ride you."

Still weak from release, she opened her mouth to speak, but he was already set on his course. He brought his cock to her still slick opening and thrust inside. Vidar made a primitive noise of satisfaction as her pussy accepted him.

Wildly, he fucked her, biting his lips as he watched her breasts bounce around with each thrust. The hard sex caused little jolts of pain deep inside her sex, but the instant pleasure following it more than made up for any discomfort. His gorgeous muscles tightened and flexed, captivating her as her breasts did him.

He grabbed a breast and squeezed, pinching the nipple between two fingers. Tension shot throughout her entire being. His mouth opened wide and she knew he held back. "Finish for me," he demanded. "Give me my prize."

Karre came, hitting her zenith with a gentle cry of relief. Seconds later he froze over her, staying buried as he met with release. With a deep, almost pained sigh, he collapsed next to her and pulled her hot body against his even hotter chest. Grabbing a breast in his palm, he closed his eyes. "I am well satisfied. My lady may have whatever she desires."

The pleasure of release diminished some at his words. He'd meant it as a compliment, but it left her feeling a little bit like a whore being paid for services. She thought about inching away from him but she was too tired to move.

5

Because right now, in this moment, her ass hurt too much.

Karre gritted her teeth, trying to think of anything but the endless rocking of the horse beneath her. Dissatisfied with her white gown, Vidar had given her a man's tunic and breeches. It suited her just fine, as she bunched the gown beneath her butt to cushion the ride.

Their morning started early, before the sun even deigned to shine down upon the waking soldiers. Vidar awoke before her, eating his breakfast before coming to massage her awake with his hands on her naked breasts. But there had been no time to finish what he started as the sound of cart wheels squeaked outside. For the first mile or so, the feel of his body tempted her desires, but now she just wanted to slip off the horse and never move again because right now, in this moment, her ass hurt too much. The sensation in her backside went from numb to burning to sharp jolts of pain to a combination of all three.

"You said I could have whatever I wanted." Karre leaned forward to whisper up into Vidar's ear. She had told herself she wasn't going to cash in on his sexual "payment" but she couldn't take anymore.

"Are you hungry?" he asked, reaching down to his leg where a satchel hung.

"No, I wish to walk."

"We are very close to—"

"Please, Vidar. I am not used to riding."

"Of course, my lady." He shouted a command to one of his men, urging them to continue on. Their horse stopped. When they were alone, Vidar swung down and reached up to help her to the ground. Her legs wobbled and she placed her hand on the horse's side to steady herself. Vidar took her by her arm. "Can you walk?"

Karre nodded, trying not to limp as she stretched her legs.

Vidar made a small clicking noise and led her

forward on the worn path. The horse followed behind them.

"You said before that Divinity traded the brides," Karre said, wanting to take her mind off her aches. Learning of yet another Divinity crime might make this detour worth it.

"Yea."

"What for?" She threaded her hand on his arm, but only because she needed to steady herself. As the cart squeaked and horse hooves softened with distance, the surrounding forest's gentle noises became apparent. The light hum of insects mingled with the slightly louder call of distant birds. In the illumination of late day, the new spring leaves seemed to glow. Tiny veins threaded them in imperfect symmetry as they crashed and danced above in the trees, taunting their fallen, brown brethren on the forest floor below.

"Water," he stated simply.

Karre stopped walking and dropped his arm. "Water? I was traded for water? Are you joking?"

"No. The Divinity aliens wanted some of the blue mineral water and offered us brides in return." He gave a small laugh. "They had great talks about the matter until finally King Wilhelm agreed to give them one small vial per bride."

As he moved on, the horse's head neared her back. She took several fast steps before falling into a leisurely pace beside him. "A vial of water. I am worth a small vial of water. That's insulting. Is it at least a cure for age? Or some kind of miracle water? Is it an elixir that makes you men big and strong when you drink it?"

"No, most would not say it is magic and we do not drink it unless desperate. It can make you sick. Though, it is blue."

"Oh great, you can't drink it but at least it's a pretty color. Decorators and spa owners everywhere will be so happy." She gave a wry laugh. The insult was too much. She remembered the henchmen had given her a bowl of such water to clean up with at Battlewar. She had thought it was mixed with some kind of soap for cleaning.

Brides for bathing water. Wonderful. Even her thoughts dripped with sarcasm.

"If it cheers you, the water is special. It stays warm no matter how long it stays away from heat. It has saved men from the cold." He swung his hand over his head and smacked a low branch.

Karre laughed dryly, stating, "Oh yes, that makes me feel much better."

They walked in silence and slowly the feeling

returned to her backside. She breathed deeply, taking in the fresh forest air. It had been so long since she'd had time to relax and enjoy a simple walk. Reaching a fallen log across the path, she started to step over it. Vidar's hand was instantly on her arm, helping her over.

"Have you ever traveled to another plane?" She'd originally meant the question as a way to start a conversation, but as she said the words she realized the strategic cunningness of it. If he had traveled, she'd find out how.

"No. Before Divinity, people only came through the fairy rings. Since we're always at war, fairies do not like our land and they do not leave rings for us to travel through." He didn't let go of her as they cleared the log. "But since I was a boy, I've been fascinated by the idea of other worlds. I love hearing the stories of such strange places."

"Where is the Divinity portal?" she asked. "Perhaps I could take you to another world? I know of some nice ones. We wouldn't be gone long. Think of it as a vacation."

"No." The answer was flat and the lightness of his tone faded. "I cannot leave the borderlands. There is much to be done."

"Oh?"

"How about you? How many planes have you traveled to?" he asked instead of elaborating.

Countless. Hundreds. Hundreds of hundreds.

"A few." Karre pulled her arm from his grasp under the pretense of stretching. When she finished, she dropped her arm to the side, putting distance between their bodies. The ground squished beneath her feet and she grimaced as cold, wet earth clung to her short boot. "Ew."

"And the world you are from?" He offered his arm so she might steady herself as she swiped at her foot. "Is it like this one?"

"No. It's nothing like this one." Karre gave up on the mud and wiped her hands on the ends of her borrowed tunic shirt. Dirt smudged over the red.

"Is it—?"

"I don't hear the knights," she interrupted so he couldn't probe more into her home plane. Turning her full attention to him, she stepped into his path, forcing him to stop walking. "We have the forest to ourselves."

"Are you not sore from the ride?" Vidar's words might have held a hint of denial, but his eyes lit with interest.

"Come with me," she pulled him off the path into the trees, gripping his tunic in her fist. The horse began to follow, but Vidar made a noise and the beast stopped, instead grazing alongside the path.

"I wish to speak—"

"Here is good." Karre slid the hand on his chest up, pulling the material to expose the laces at his waist. With a deft tug, she untied them.

He looked as if he might protest the quickness of her advances. "My lady, I—*ah!*"

Karre tugged his pants down to his knees, letting them slide the rest of the way to trap his ankles. His cock had started to rise with interest and she cupped the shaft, stroking the length until it firmed against her palm. She licked her lips, dragging her tongue leisurely as he watched.

All questions left his eyes as he gave in. Karre smiled, took the hem of his tunic and bunched it by his chest, out of her way. "Hold this."

His hand pressed flat, holding it up. Karre sank to her knees, scratching her nails against his hips. He tensed, threading his fingers into her hair, rubbing along her temple insistently. Looking up at him, she kept her eyes on his as she leaned forward. Her lips parted, slipping around the wide tip of his erection. Vidar's breathing deepened.

Karre worked her mouth down his length, sucking gently. He groaned in satisfaction. His eyes closed as he tilted his head back in rapture. She rolled her tongue along his shaft, all the while running her nails down the backs of his thighs. His strong abdomen muscles rippled beneath his flesh. He rocked in time with her mouth. She felt him quiver and reached for his balls. Almost instantly, he jerked, coming inside her mouth. Swallowing, she let his cock slide from her lips.

Vidar breathed heavily, his hand dropping from her hair. He lowered to the ground, joining her. Crawling forward, he forced her onto her back. He brushed his lips against hers. "My turn."

He tugged at her laces, pulling her breeches free. Then, eagerly, he dipped his head between her thighs, as if he'd been waiting all day to taste her. He moaned, the sound vibrating her clit. He licked along her pussy, sucking, biting, thrusting his tongue inside her.

Her ass pressed into dry leaves and the crunching sound of their destruction punctuated each movement. Vidar massaged her hips with his hands, rocking them up toward his mouth. Karre gripped his head. Tension built, filling her with a bittersweet agony. She wanted the sensations to last forever, but she couldn't stop the rough jerk of release that washed over her.

When the last tremors subsided, Vidar looked up and gave her a satisfied grin. "The fortress is close." His pants still bound his ankles and he pulled them up as he stood. "There, we can bathe and dine." He reached to pull her up. "And find you an appropriate gown."

"You SAID the fortress was close, I had no idea it was only a hundred-pace walk. Why didn't you insist we finish the ride?"

Vidar watched his wife from the corner of his eye. Behind them, his horse walked a lazy pace without having to be led. "Because you asked me to stop and it was within my power to grant you the simple request. Oskar will see that everything is taken care of in my stead."

Though small compared to the great city of Battlewar, Spearhead had a symmetrical charm—for a fortress on the brink of a vicious Caniba attack. A single watchtower lifted high into the sky, lording over the square-shaped castle beneath. Thorn hedges formed a perimeter around the outside wall, surrounded by the murky waters of a moat. Vidar kept an eye on Karre, wondering what she thought of her new home. Surely, the sight would impress her.

"Sir Vidar!" yelled a knight from atop the battlements, announcing Vidar's arrival to those behind the stronghold's wall. "And Lady Karre!"

"Rejoice, Sir Vidar has chosen!" a woman near the front gate shouted, prompting a chorus of others to join her. "Rejoice! Rejoice, Sir Vidar has chosen!"

Karre stiffened at the words, her face tightening. He watched a strange expression filter over her, first shock, then resolve, fading to determination. Glancing in his direction, her determination was replaced by a light smile. But he studied her eyes and their intensity was nowhere near the lighthearted emotion she wanted him to believe.

Taking her arm, he led her over the bridge and through the opened front gates. The raised stone of the bailey wall surrounded the courtyard, looping about from one side of the main castle to the other in an oval shape. Atop the wall that stood several feet wide was the walkway surrounded by battlements with corner spiral stairwells leading from the ground to the battlements. Next to the tower, the main part of Spearhead Fortress sprawled along the backside of the wall.

The wide courtyard teemed with activity, just

like Battlewar City but on a smaller scale. Unlike Battlewar, Spearhead had no market, no tightly pressed homes filling tiny streets, but there was a self-sustaining brewery and gardens for food. Livestock was tended in the north, the meat part of the supplies they brought back with them.

Now, the movement stopped as those gathered cheered the new couple. Two guards pushed the oversized doors of the main gate closed and secured them with a thick timber. Karre whistled lightly. When Vidar looked at her, she said, "This will do."

He grinned with pride and excitement. "Welcome to your home, my lady."

"WELCOME HOME INDEED." Karre gave a wry laugh as she looked around her new bedchamber. It was adequate in size with pale stone walls, a smoothed stone floor, large stone fireplace and a stone bench carved beneath a narrow stone window. "This is exactly like the time I spent a month trapped in a cave because Lopa-lis were after me."

Okay, so it wasn't *exactly* like the cave. It did have furnishings.

"My lady?"

Karre turned to Jordinne, the maid Vidar assigned to assist her while he left for some mysterious duty. She was a pretty girl, youthful in appearance and temperament. She suited Karre just fine. Youth was easier to manipulate. "I asked if it would be possible to have a bath. You do bathe here, right? They gave me a bowl of water at Battlewar when I would much prefer a tub or shower. Even a waterfall would do."

"Yea, my lady, we bathe," Jordinne giggled. "But here in Spearhead we do not dress as men—not like those heathen ladies of a Battlewar."

Like every other woman Karre had seen in Spearhead, the servant wore a long flowing dress cinched tight with a corset top that dipped low to lay bare a fair amount of cleavage. Karre wondered if Jordinne had ever seen a woman from Battlewar, because when Karre had been there she'd not seen a single lady there dressed as a man.

Well, she thought, looking at her own clothes, *no one but myself.*

"Yes, they eo seem a barbaric lot compared to this place," Karre agreed to win the woman over. It worked. Jordinne's smile widened. "And with your great enemy so close, it is a great accomplishment to remain so civil."

Jordinne nodded enthusiastically. "Yea, my lady."

"I require a bath," Karre said, slipping comfortably into her new role. If this plane demanded she play the part of Lady Karre of Spearhead, so be it. She had pretended to be a lady of means before. "I will also need gowns and shoes worthy of Spearhead as well as sturdy clothes for riding. Food and drink."

Karre again looked around the stone tomb of her chamber. One door led out of the room, opening up to Vidar's bedchambers. She'd been informed that noble women did not sleep with their husband throughout the night. The large bed dominated Karre's room and had been covered with a decorative fur, but the muted browns and grays of the sewn squares only added to the overall drabness.

"And, if possible," she continued, "I need some material samples, some lightweight chain or rope, someone who can sew, a couple swords, a knife or dagger. Hmm, actually, you'd better have several weapons sent up for my inspection."

Jordinne watched her, not moving.

Karre sighed. "See to it, please."

"Yea, my lady." Jordinne nodded and hurried from the room, her eyes deep in concentration.

Karre relaxed and tugged at her clothing, stripping out of the traveling garb. Completely naked, she crawled onto the bed and under the fur covers. The soft mattress molded to her body, cushioning her sore muscles. She moaned, content for the moment. Maybe the chamber wasn't so bad after all.

KARRE AWOKE HOURS LATER, rested and incredibly aroused from endless dreams filled with the wicked temptation of Vidar's masculine body. In her sleep, she had pulled the covers off her chest, revealing her naked breasts. Sitting up, she found that someone had been in to light the fire.

Karre pulled the blanket up to quickly hide herself as she looked around. The room was empty. The clothing she had discarded earlier was gone, replaced by a neatly folded gown on the end of her bed. A tray carrying a trencher of meats and bread was left on a low table next to a goblet. Leaning from the bed, she grabbed the goblet and took a long drink of the sweet liquor before setting the empty goblet back down with a sigh.

She didn't like the fact that someone had come in while she slept—let alone spent enough time to light a fire, deliver laundry and bring in food. It wasn't like her mind to let down its guard. She would have to take more care in the future.

By the light coming through the window, she knew the hour was late. Karre kicked off the fur. The room was warm and her flushed skin nearly glowed in the firelight. A bath had been left near the fire, the blue water warm and inviting when she skimmed her fingers over the surface. Instead of stepping into the metal tub, she went to the door. The tub was small, but she would find a way to fit Vidar in there with her, even if she had to sit on his lap—*especially* if she had to sit on his lap.

His room was empty. Glancing over the sparse décor just to be sure, she frowned. Shouldn't he have come back from his duties by now? She had a hard time believing that a man of his passions would have checked in on her and left her to sleep.

Disappointed, she left the door open and went to her bath. Heat caressed every inch beneath the surface of the mineral water. She lifted her arm, watching the blue droplets rain down from her fingers like liquid sapphires. On the floor next to her, she found sweet smelling soaps. She took her time, watching the open door, waiting for Vidar to come in and catch her naked in the tub.

Karre soaped her breasts before standing to wash

her stomach and thighs. The lather caused her hands to slip pleasurably over her form and she bit her lip. Images of Vidar invaded her senses—strong, sexy, erotic, masturbating as he faced the wall. She smiled, her knees weakening as she sank back into the water.

Karre leaned her head back, rubbing her soapy breasts while reaching between her thighs. She massaged her clit, rubbing it in small circles. Lazy eyes stayed fixed on the door, willing him to come to her. She pressed harder. He didn't come to her and she couldn't hold off the tremors of release.

"LORD RONEN's man has arrived. He informs me that they have recovered Lady Jayne from the forest. She was abducted by Caniba scouts," Sir Oskar said, joining Vidar along the low ridge. Moss-covered trees lined the wetlands, beyond the shallow waters that surrounded the island hill of their new encampment. Patches of vegetation grew in the water, forming a random pattern in the surface. It was the perfect location, almost pretty but for the stale air of the surrounding marshlands that settled thickly in their lungs, carrying the faint scent of death. "He brings a missive from the king."

Vidar looked from the mossy trees to Oskar's hand, taking the letter. "She made it to the borderlands, then?"

"No. They were discovered near Widowsrock." Oskar's frown mirrored Vidar's.

"That far north? In the forest?" He broke the wax seal, not looking at the letter as he stared at Oskar for confirmation.

"Yea, but that is all I know. The man would tell me no more, only insisted on my honor that I bring this to you."

Vidar hurriedly unfolded the parchment to find two pages. He read over them quickly. "King Wilhelm says Sorceress Magda's men were caught with maps of Staria. They are charting routes through the forest originating at Spearhead and heading north toward Battlewar and Fallenrock. The king urges me to renew efforts to find the sorceress. Everything he has is at our disposal. He sends troops to reinforce the borderlands and the forests."

"Sorceress Magda has yet to show herself. All we have are rumors that she is even near here." Oscar took the first page of the missive when Vidar offered it to him. They had shared much and owed each other their lives more than either of them could count. "For all we know she could be five miles underground and fifty miles from the border."

"She must be close. I feel it like an oncoming sickness—close but not quite within reach." Vidar turned, looking in the direction of his fortress. It was impossible to see it from where he was, but he imagined it perfectly. Lady Karre would be there, settling into her new home, her new life. He thought of writing her but had not found the time to put pen to paper. Now, with news of Magda's daring, he would have even less time for it.

Besides, what would he say with no news of battle to speak of? Should anything happen to him, she'd be informed by one of his men so simply saying "I'm alive" seemed pointless. Perhaps she wasn't concerned. Perhaps she was. Perhaps she didn't think of him at all.

She is probably too busy to give me more than a passing thought. Though the most likely scenario, he found the idea bothered him somewhat.

Shaking his bride from his thoughts with great effort, he sighed and turned to the rectangular tents outlined by firelight in the coming dusk. Tiny sparks from the flames danced in the evening sky before dying out. The tents, varying in sizes, spread out over the high clearing on an orderly grid to create pathways. The larger tents were in the middle with progressively smaller ones fanning round them. Banners hung from the tent flaps, pinned to the opened entryways. Their brilliant colors stuck out against the light caramel of the canvas.

"It says here that the map did not go too far into the forest. They could not have been spying long," Oskar pointed out. "He wants a report as to our progress. What will you tell him?"

"What can I tell him?" Vidar muttered, feeling a little bitter. "That his sending me to Battlewar for a bride left Spearhead open? That Caniba spies broke through the forest near my fortress? I can't even be certain when they snuck through. This is the first I've heard of it."

Oskar did not offer any words of comfort and Vidar did not expect any. "You needed a bride and now you've got one. There will be no need to leave Spearhead again. You followed the king's orders."

"Read the rest of it." Vidar handed him the second page.

"Sir Vidar," Oskar read aloud, "I have been informed that the Divinity brides might not have known about coming to our land. Already Lord Sorin and Lord Ronen have expressed discontentment from their wives. Let us hope it is nervousness from traveling to a new land, but if it is more than that, we must do all in our power to ensure these first marriages stand. I do not want marital chaos in my kingdom, especially amongst my noblemen. We need this trade agreement with the foreigners to work. More brides means more children. Within a generation we will have more knights to defend this kingdom. Already the Caniba outnumber us by at least threefold. Then, gods willing, maybe this war will end and we will wipe the beastly scourge from existence. I should like to be remembered as the king whose actions started the downfall of our enemy."

Vidar's stomach tightened with worry. How was he to look after a woman and see to his warrior duties? Marriage was supposed to ease the stress of life, not add to it.

"You are a man of great honor, sir," Oskar continued reading, his voice lowering. "I expect you to find happiness in your marriage. I will not have the trade agreement tarnished by rumors of the gods being angered with us for trying to take more brides than they readily bestow. The knights need a reason to fight and the hope of a lady always seems to be the best motivation. I am not ready to give up on this alliance. Do whatever you must and learn what you can of your wife's presence at the breeding ceremony. Keep this news to yourself. I have no wish to dampen the spirits of the men with Sorceress Magda threatening our borders."

Oskar handed the letter back and Vidar folded it only to clutch it in his hand. He knew his orders, contradicting as they were. He needed to stop Magda and ensure his wife's happiness. Though, the last shouldn't be hard. It was unfortunate Sorin and Ronen had not found peace in their marriages, but Karre seemed happy to be with him.

"Do we ride for Spearhead?" Oskar asked.

"Not yet." No. No matter how badly he wanted to go to his wife, to feel her against him, he was needed at the marsh encampment. "I have left orders to be informed should my wife need anything. There is nothing to worry about. The maids will see to Lady Karre and ensure she is taken care of. Besides, I have prisoners to interrogate."

Two warriors had fallen, Richard of Daggerpoint and Peeter of Fallenrock, while capturing some of Sorceress Magda's scouts in the southern marshes. With her people popping up everywhere, something big was close. He could feel it in his bones. The fallen Starian men could have killed the Caniba warriors and lived, but both men knew their duty and knew that they needed live prisoners for information.

They died well and were not taken by the cannibals. After several weeks without their queen, Vidar hoped the scouts would be ready to talk. Caniba warriors became erratic and unpredictably mad when withdrawn from their idol.

"Let us hope that tonight is the night we discover where the sorceress' encampment lies." Vidar led the way up the incline toward the tent village.

6

Because right now, in this moment, she didn't care if she found anything worthy of hawking for a portal ride, she needed to get the hell out of Spearhead Fortress.

"It is whispered that Sorceress Magda studies the black arts. Her followers dance with the serpent and are made to endure its poison before joining her army. Only those who live, the toughest of the Caniba, are allowed into her ranks." Jordinne paused in her story, looking at the other two maids gathered in Karre's bedchamber. The maids sat in thickly cushioned chairs, newly padded as per Karre's design. Richly colored fabrics hung from the walls to hide the stone underneath, flowing red and golds. Matching fabric hung around the bed, creating opulent curtains, held open with corded ropes. Firelight shone from the fireplace, contrasting their faces, exaggerating their expressions.

Karre took a deep breath, trying not to shiver. She hadn't moved for some time from her place lounging on the bed. Vidar had been gone for weeks, leaving her to make her way in Spearhead alone. He'd just dropped her off and left. The fact stung, but she refused to dwell on it as she busied herself with familiarizing herself with the fortress and the people in it. She played the role they demanded, though it was tougher than other identities she had taken. They all called her Karre and she wasn't sure what kind of character to be under her real name. She didn't even know how to be her real self. Characters were much easier.

Karre had searched for valuables, something portable she could carry with her when she discovered a way off this plane. The weapons inspection brought little more than sharp blades and used swords. Bolts of material were nice, but they wouldn't travel easily. And, as far as she could see, the fortress had no treasury. However, that was beginning to matter less and less as the women spoke.

Because right now, in this moment, she didn't care if she found anything worthy of hawking for a portal ride, she needed to get the hell out of Spearhead Fortress.

"And these Caniba are close to Spearhead even now?" Karre asked, thinking of the man-eaters the Starian people described in morbid detail—hairy, foul-smelling, beast-warriors with eyes pitted deep into their faces, sharpened teeth to bite into their awful meals and flesh covered with so many dirty pelts it looked as if they had fur.

"Yea," Jordinne nodded. "Right on the border. Over the last four years, Magda has been getting very close to Spearhead and her warriors more aggressive in battle. Or at least that is what our men tell us."

"And you stay here willingly?" Karre searched every one of their faces. Each set of eyes looked back at her as if she'd just asked them the stupidest possible question. "Why not move north where it is safer?"

"Our men will protect us," Jordinne said calmly.

"And if they don't?" Karre gasped in disbelief. "Or if they can't? What will you do then?"

"To say such a thing is..." Jordinne's weak voice trailed off.

"It's dishonorable," the redheaded Bratene answered, her green eyes wide in her round head.

"It was just a question," Karre whispered, seeing their mounting irritation at her doubtful words. She didn't need to make enemies of the women.

"Those men, the strongest of the beasts, live only to serve her, obsessively doing the sorceress' biding," Jordinne said quickly, as if trying to gloss over Karre's improper question. Her words filled with the drama of her tale. "They go mad when they can't see her. I've seen it happen to a prisoner once. They cry and yell and pull out their hair."

Karre had asked them to tell her of the Caniba but did not expect the tales of horror and depravity that they spun for her like youngsters around a campfire.

"The Caniba rise from the earth and disappear like ghosts," Bratene added.

"It's impossible to tell Magda's numbers," Synna said, her words as soft as her sweet demeanor. She tugged shyly at her brown curly hair. "Her armies sleep beneath the earth, in the ground."

"They hibernate like snakes," Bratene broke in, "but are the children of men and wolves. Wolf-men."

Dancing as Sparkle, Karre had seen several wolf-men. Sure they drank blood, but they'd been harmless enough. But had they turned evil and attacked, she could see how claws and fangs would make for a fearsome opponent.

"My first husband, Sir Fredrick, was one of the men who tried to infiltrate her camp," Synna continued as if Bratene hadn't interrupted. "He came back, but was never the same since being held as her prisoner. They have him locked away in a room lined with mattresses to keep him from bashing his own skull against the stone walls as he cries for the presence of the sorceress. I don't know what she did to him, but he is no longer my husband. He eats without utensils or plate and a man must watch him at all times to be sure he does not hurt himself or escape." Synna gave a small sniff and rubbed at her eyes. "I shall never see him again."

Jordinne leaned over to pat Synna's leg gently. "The gods will reward him well in the afterlife. Take comfort that you have other husbands."

Synna nodded but said no more.

"The Caniba are beasts, a race born of the unholy fornications of people and wolves," Bratene insisted, repeating her earlier words. This time she stared at Karre, as if to make sure she heard.

"Those are just children's stories," Jordinne denied. "You know better than to scare Lady Karre with those tales. Our men have fought and killed many in battle. They are flesh and blood."

"They are the lowest form a man can become," Bratene said.

"Be that as it may." Jordinne sighed heavily.

"It is why we all carry a knife," Bratene said lifting her skirts to show her upper thigh. A sheathed blade had been strapped tightly to her leg. "For if we are ever taken, we know what needs to be done."

"But I thought you said the men would protect us," Karre couldn't help saying, testing their earlier logic.

"They will," Bratene inserted quickly. "Of course they will."

"We trust our men to be honorable," Jordinne added.

Then why carry the knife at all?

Karre gave a nervous laugh, one she didn't feel.

"But if the gods so choose," Bratene said carefully, lightly touching her throat.

"Yea, if the gods so choose," Jordinne reiterated.

"You should carry one as well," Synna said, "just in case the gods so choose."

Karre studied them each in turn, taking in their earnest expression, reading more there than they would ever say. At their expectancy, she nodded once.

Yeah, Karre thought derisively, *if the gods so choose.*

It was time to get out of Spearhead Fortress and head north. Usually Karre wasn't one for taking off into an alien plane's wilderness on her own, but desperate times called for a desperate Karre to grab whatever she could find and run far away from the people-eating monsters. This wasn't her fight. She already had a great adversary—Divinity Corporation —and it was an all-consuming, vile foe. She didn't battle beasts with a simple blade for protection. Even a forest filled with mammoth wolves, wild boar and charging bucks was preferable to wolf-men cannibals.

Karre felt her thigh, where the maids insisted she keep a knife hidden. They'd given her a sheath that tied around her waist on top and around her thigh on the bottom to hold the knife in place. The weight was a constant reminder of what was out there.

Our men will protect us.

Jordinne had been so certain. That was well and

good for them, but Karre's man hadn't been seen or heard from in weeks—and she did not count Sir Oskar's few mumbled sentences when he'd stopped by the fortress as word from her husband. Apparently, Vidar was at a marshland encampment seeing to his "duty". No wife, on any plane, would put up with the duty excuse.

Good thing I'm not really a wife.

Striding through Vidar's chambers, she didn't bother to look around. She had already snooped through his belongings. Aside from clothes and weapons, there was nothing noteworthy.

Outside the chamber, she slowed her steps, keeping her feet soft on the stone. She'd had the seamstress sew her a bag. Its strap fitted over her chest and the large bag hung alongside her hip. Inside, trinkets she had collected were padded with bits of material to keep them from clanking as she walked. She'd also wrapped foodstuffs for the journey.

She wasn't scared, not of this, not of stealing out of a castle in the middle of the night. Over the last week, activity seemed to increase in the fortress. Knights came and went, always armed and sometimes covered in blood as they rode into the castle, always grim-faced and determined when they rode out. Tension tightened the lines of those who stayed behind.

Karre had been in some pretty rough situations, but wolf-men who ate their victims? The images it conjured made her stomach curl and the nightmares were even worse.

Our men will protect us.

"Then where the hell is my great protector?" Karre took a deep breath, trying to convince herself she didn't care that Vidar was gone. Why should she? They had only known each other a short time before he left. So what if her body still desired him? So what if in her nightmares it was always him coming to save her? So what if in the dreams that followed they made love—tender and sweet, hard and rough, bent over tables, pressed against trees, in the dining hall at his place of honor, on the battlements, in the brewery... Okay, so there wasn't a place in the fortress she hadn't dreamed of being with him in.

She forced her mind to clear until only the task at hand filtered through her thoughts. Walking down the darkened hall, she ran the back of her hand over the stone to keep on path. Twenty steps would take her to her turn, then another twenty-three until she reached the main hall. Hopefully, with the late hour, no one would be there.

Karre quickened her pace, going through the arched doorway to the main hall where everyone gathered to dine during the day and drink generous amounts of liquor in the evening. Drinking would lead to fornicating and the people of Spearhead didn't always retire to their chambers when it came time to "play".

Scanning the long rows of tables littered with goblets, she found one couple sleeping on top of one at the far side of the room near the large fireplace. Karre walked to the head table, where she dined with a few of the honored knights, and grabbed an etched metal goblet. Shoving it in her bag, she reached for another one, dumping the remaining liquor on the floor. When she'd taken all five of the etched ones, she made her way toward the entrance with her hand on the bag to keep the goblets from clanking.

Her foot stepped on something in the dim light. She gasped, looking down to find a retracting hand disappearing beneath a table.

"Hold, watch it," someone mumbled.

She stiffened, waiting several seconds before moving. The person's hand did not reappear. Letting out her captured breath, she renewed her pace.

The chill of early morning brought with it a strange silence. The courtyard normally bustled with activity, but now it was abandoned and desolate. Faint shafts of light streaked the sky, but it was still too early for the sun to rise. Stars shone bright and she looked up to get her bearings. On most planes the constellations remained the same and once you could read them, it was possible to navigate no matter where you were—so long as you could see the sky.

She neared the front gate, looking up at the battlements. The guards walked the length four times an hour throughout the night, circling back behind the castle. With no man guarding the gate, she took the steps leading up the outer bailey wall. She couldn't unlatch the gate without drawing attention, but she could climb down the side of the wall onto the pathway from the gate to beyond the moat. With luck, no one would spot her escape.

Karre took off the bag and lifted it up, ready to swing it over the side. The sound of approaching hooves caused her to draw back her hand at the last moment, clanging the goblets as she clutched the bag to her stomach.

"Ho! Open the gate!"

Vidar!

Shit!

"Identify yourself!" Vidar demanded when she didn't move. She could see by the silhouette of his body that he was looking up at her. Karre ducked down, hiding from view as she went to the narrow stairs to climb off the wall. The sound of running feet came as a guard made his way to investigate.

Vidar came home now? After weeks of being gone? It was a cruel twist of irony that he arrived the exact moment she tried to leave him. A shiver worked over her at the thought and she looked at the sky. It couldn't be...

If the gods so choose.

Vidar shouted behind her as she ran from the wall, but the words were distorted. The gate creaked open behind her and Vidar rode in. "Karre?"

She stopped moving. There was no point in running now. Slowly, she turned, watching the horse come to a stop. A knight closed the main gate behind him as another from atop the wall watched the scene below. As the man by the gate came to take Vidar's horse, Vidar strode the remaining distance toward her.

Think, Karre, think. Come up with an excuse. Smile at him.

"What are you doing on the wall, my lady?" he asked, his handsome brow furrowed.

She had forgotten how good he looked. The golden flecks in his hazel eyes caught up the moonlight, casting an animalistic, primal charm about him. Memories of his hands, how they felt, of his warm lips running over her flesh filled her. Her nerves tingled, as if reaching out to him.

"Looking," she managed to answer after some time.

"Looking for what?"

Think of something.

She hugged the bag tighter. Weakly, she said, "For the Caniba."

His questioning expression turned hard. "Caniba? Have they been spotted near the gate? Why wasn't I informed? Get inside at once!" He reached for the sword at his waist and began to turn around to chase after the guard.

"No, they haven't," Karre said, stopping him. "The maids told me stories and I... It's silly. I think I scared myself and I just had to see the countryside for myself to make sure they weren't out there."

He looked at her again with piercing intensity and she lost her breath. Her eyes traveled down over his form—moving over his broad chest to his waist. Seeing the knife hanging near his hip, her eyes moved back up.

"I couldn't sleep," she finished, patting the blade hidden by her skirts.

At that, he relaxed. "There is no reason to be scared. Every man here would lay down his life to protect you, my lady."

And if they fail?

Vidar reached to cup her cheek. "You look worried."

"Sleepy," she mumbled. An awkward moment passed between them. He withdrew his hand and averted his eyes to the entrance behind her. The breeze shifted and she smelled the dried perspiration on his body, mingled with horse and dirt. "Should we go in?"

Vidar nodded. Karre looked at the wall, thinking of how close she'd come to escaping this place. But with Vidar there, the urge to run dissipated, replaced by the need to touch him, hear him, taste him. When he touched her, she felt safe, as if that brief contact could melt away all her worry.

"Will you wake a servant to bring me a bath?" he asked, falling into step beside her.

"Yes." Her breathing deepened. Vidar in a bath, naked, wet.

"Thank you, my lady. I am weary from the ride." He reached to take her satchel. "Let me take this to your chamber for you."

Karre snatched it back in surprise. The goblets

banged together. Vidar stopped walking and arched a brow. Panicking, she dropped the bag and lifted her arms around his neck, kissing him hard. His lips tensed and he gasped in surprise, but her insistent tongue to his mouth forced him to relax.

She let her body mold to his, feeling a tingling pressure where they touched. Karre moaned, momentarily forgetting herself. Vidar placed his hands on her hips and pushed her firmly back. "Let us go inside."

Karre grabbed her bag and used his words as an excuse to carry it herself. "I'll see to your bath."

AFTER WAKING a servant and putting her stolen goblets back on the table, Karre hurried back to the chambers she shared with Vidar. Her heart beat fast, with both the idea of almost being caught and the promise of Vidar's seduction. By the time she reached his bedchamber door, she was breathing heavily.

Without knocking, she went inside. To her surprise, she found Bratene leaning over Vidar in the metal tub, scrubbing his naked back. Vidar moaned, a low, throaty sound of pleasure.

Karre skidded to a stop, her mouth opening. For a long moment, she didn't say anything as she waited for them to notice her. The servant lifted his arm, washing his side. Karre crossed her arms over chest, still waiting to be noticed. Bratene's hands dipped beneath the water, following the indent of his spine down, down, down...

"Stop right there," Karre demanded loudly.

Bratene gasped and jerked away from Vidar. The maid's eyes were wide when she turned to Karre. Vidar glanced back, his movements slow. She expected remorse or guilt, instead he just looked.

"Out," she ordered Bratene.

"But I have not finished," the maid protested.

"Out," Karre repeated with more force. "Now."

Vidar's brows lowered over his gorgeous eyes.

"My lady," Bratene mumbled, rushing out of the door.

When it slammed closed, Vidar said, "She wasn't finished."

"What? Washing you?" Karre stormed across the room to her door, going into her chambers to hide her bag before coming back to face him. "I thought men of Staria did not sleep with other women once they were married."

"What are you talking about?" Vidar frowned.

"Perhaps the word sleep was too vague," she answered, pacing past his tub only to turn around and pace back so she could face him. Hands on hips, she continued, "You said that your gods smile upon your marriages and that you do not seek to fuck other women because you have to be faithful or warlike or disciplined. War, marriage..." She slashed her hand at him, not even coming close to touching him.

"We stay faithful because the gods demand discipline," he corrected. "Just as war demands discipline. It is our way."

"Whatever," she grumbled.

"You are angry?" He made no move to get out of the bath and the firelight reflection on the glistening water that beaded on his soap-trailed flesh made her mouth go dry.

"What do I care if the maid tries to..." She gestured at his chest. A thought whispered in the back of her mind that she needed to stop talking, needed to walk away, needed to rethink what she was doing. This conversation wasn't calculated or planned and it definitely was not advantageous. "I mean, you've been gone. You..." She hesitated at his piercing look. "You didn't tell me you were going."

The argument seemed silly now that it was said.

"You are upset because I left without speaking

with you first?" He straightened. "I told you I had duties to attend to and I sent word with Sir Oskar."

Oh, yes, the mumbling Sir Oskar. How did the knight put it? "My lady, Sir Vidar sends his respect. He is detained at the marshland encampment. Have you a message for him?"

"I was not told you needed me while I was away," he added.

Why was he looking at her like that?

"What do I care if you leave? You don't owe me an explanation. We only knew each other a few days before you left." Karre frowned. And that was it. The truth of it. The whole of their relationship. A few short days, a ceremony and a small trip. She had no reason to say the things coming out of her mouth. She had no reason to be jealous of Bratene.

Oh, but she was jealous. Her entire body seethed with it. The emotion struck her hard, forcing her to act without thought. And it was not only jealousy, but anger and frustration that he left her, his bride, alone in a strange fortress threatened by cannibals. She didn't ask to marry him, didn't plan to stay married to him, for such a thing would never work, but he didn't know that.

"Then you are jealous that Bratene bathed me? There is no reason. It is a servant's job to bathe—"

"Well, I made some changes while you were gone," Karre interrupted, well aware of how she sounded but unable to stop. "I can work, too, you know."

He smiled and there was a definite challenge in his gold-flecked gaze. "Changes to bathing?"

"Yes. No. I mean we still bathe. Of course there will still be bathing. But maids don't bathe married men." Karre knelt by the tub and reached her hand behind him. Finding the washcloth the maid had dropped, she pushed it onto his back. The warm heat radiating off him and the subtle smell of Starian soap caused her to inhale deeply. "I can bathe you and, if I'm not around, you can do it yourself."

"But servants—"

"Yourself." Karre pushed at his back. Bathing servants weren't unheard of in her travels, but neither were the "happy endings" they included with the deal. "No maids are to be massaging any part of you while I'm around."

"Very well, my lady, it will be as you wish."

"Good." She nodded, moving to methodically scrub his back. "I'm glad we understand each other."

7

Because right now, in this moment, she didn't want to think.

Karre massaged Vidar's neck, having discarded the washcloth to use her hands. Soap made her fingers glide over the solid ridge of muscles and she took full advantage of his wet, naked state. She explored every inch under the guise of washing him. Her thighs tightened and her pussy ached to be filled as moisture gathered along the soft folds.

She pulled, urging him to lean back in the metal tub. Small protests erupted in her mind, but she willfully refused to heed them because right now, in this moment, she didn't want to think. Karre rubbed his chest, pressing her hands firmly in the center and massaging them outward. She skimmed his nipples and his breath caught.

She kept exploring, moving leisurely down until her hands dipped beneath the water. The tight hold of her green corset pulled tight to her chest, forcing her breasts up and together to create deep cleavage. Vidar stared at her breasts as she leaned over him and gripped the edge of the tub.

She found his navel and the back of her hand brushed his solid cock. Vidar groaned. Wet fingertips found her breasts and thrust between them. She wrapped her massaging fingers around his erection, gliding down to his balls, then up.

"Take off your gown," he ordered.

Karre made no move to obey. She twisted her hands on his cock, lacing her fingers as she worked her hands over him beneath the blue water.

"I wish to take you now," he said, not as commanding as before. "Lift your skirts and climb on top of me."

Karre ignored the request. She pumped harder, gripping him tighter. "No, I'm bathing you."

Water splashed on her sleeves and shoulders. She thrust one hand down to grab his balls and the root of his shaft while the other continued to move along the smooth arousal. The hand between her breasts tried to tug the mounds from the corset, but without loosening the laces, they were bound too tightly.

Vidar tensed, his body jerking beautifully as he came beneath the water. She kept pumping, milking his cock of every last drop. When his head fell back, she stopped, grinning. Running a finger down the center of his chest, she said, "There's a good warrior."

"Yea," Vidar breathed, his limp body hers to command. He didn't know why the maid's presence had upset her, as it was common for servants to attend a leader's bath, but he found he liked the spark of jealousy he saw in her. Besides, no maid had ever given him a bath like the one he'd just had.

Lids fell heavy over his eyes as he watched Karre stand. She began pulling at her corset and he licked his lips in eager anticipation. Glorious breasts spilled forward and the bodice dropped to the ground. The underdress had been cut low in the front, open to her waist. She pushed the wet sleeves aside, unveiling her naked form.

Vidar pushed up from the bath, stepping out. He'd missed the feel of her body. Even as his cock lay limp and satisfied, he knew it would easily be roused to go again.

Instead of dropping her gown, she walked to him, holding it before her. She used it to dry him off. He couldn't resist cupping a breast as it came within reach. He groaned, squeezing it.

Karre covered his hand with hers and pulled him with her toward his bed. She sat on the end and spread her thighs. "Kneel, warrior."

He did as she commanded, kneeling between her legs. The pink folds were parted, showcasing the hidden bud of her clit surrounded by the glistening cream of her body. Her pussy welcomed his mouth and he moaned as her taste filled him. He thrust his tongue into her before licking up her slit. She squirmed, thrusting into him. He gripped her thighs.

His cock lifted, jealous of his mouth's pleasure. He reached to pump the shaft, helping it to full capacity. Feeling how wet she was, how open, he surged to his feet. She looked at him in surprise, but he didn't wait. Bringing his arousal to her pussy, he thrust hard, pulling her body into his so they slammed together. He had to bend his knees to make their position work, but he ignored the burn in his thighs and calves as he propelled his hips back and forth.

"Oh, oh, oh," Karre gasped over and over, punctuating his thrusts with the feminine sounds. Her large breasts bobbed as she reached her hands over her head to grab the fur coverlet on his bed. He fucked her harder, just to watch them move. Oh, how he wanted to bury his face between them. How he wanted to lick them, bite them, fuck them until they were covered in his cum.

He knew he had missed being with her, but he hadn't realized how much until this moment. Her pussy trembled around his erection and her back arched off the bed. Vidar couldn't resist her body's call as she came. He jerked, meeting his climax as her muscles clamped down. With a great sigh, he collapsed to his knees and rested his head on the edge of the mattress. Her legs were still open, unmoving against his arms.

When he regained his strength, he crawled up onto the bed and lay down next to her. "Would you like me to carry you to your chamber?"

Karre gave a soft laugh. "I heard that Starian men and women don't sleep in the same bed." She pulled her legs up over the side and inched higher so their faces were close. Stroking his cheek, she said, "That's another change I'm going to make. There's no reason to sleep in separate beds. You can carry me back to my room, but only if you plan on staying there with me."

WHAT HAD SHE BEEN THINKING? Sleep in the same room? The Starian setup had been perfect, affording her privacy. Even as she knew her staunch control was slipping, she couldn't help snuggling closer to Vidar's side. The man was a machine in bed, going for hours, and incredibly enthusiastic.

After carrying her to her bed, he'd taken his time exploring her breasts—nipping, kissing, licking, fucking. He pulled her on top of him to straddle his face as he lay on his back. He'd buried his mouth and chin in her sex, only turning her around as she began to climax so she could ride his cock to completion. He bent her on her hands and knees and took her from behind, pounding into her until sweat slicked their bodies and she couldn't breathe from the sheer pleasure of it. He then turned in the bed and lay on his side, leisurely licking her pussy as she sucked his marvelous cock.

Karre believed he would have kept going had she not protested and begged to sleep. Now, as morning light streamed into the room, she felt his hard cock nudging her naked thigh. She lay on her stomach, her head turned from him. Vidar lifted her hair before brushing his lips along the back of her neck.

"I will have to thank Sir Jacque for his words. I find I enjoyed implementing his advice." Vidar nipped at her flesh while his hand skimmed over her naked ass.

Karre chuckled. "Who's he?"

"A soldier from the marsh encampment. I felt how you enjoyed such things." Fingers followed down the cleft, nearing her pussy. "There are more positions that I would like to try."

"Haven't you had enough?" She moaned in protest, only partially meaning it. Her muscles ached with the dull fatigue only a night of sex could bring.

"Of you? Not even close, my lady." Vidar pressed his hips into her. "I wish to finish you again before going to break our fast."

"Do you have to leave again?" She turned her face into the bed.

Vidar's finger wiggled its way to her clit. "Only when word from the marshland encampment calls me away."

"Why would they call you?" She parted her legs slightly to ease his way.

"I do not wish—" he began.

"How is it you wanted to take me?" She turned to him, eyeing him through her lashes.

Instantly, he pushed up. "Sit on my lap."

Karre did, straddling his legs. She smiled when his eyes instantly went to her breasts. "You were saying? Why would they call you away?"

"I do—" Vidar gasped as she pushed her breasts into his face only to withdraw. "I interrogated Magda's spies while I was there." Karre did it again, twisting so her nipple hit his mouth. He sucked it into his mouth and groaned. She pulled back and the nipple slipped from his grasp with a loud *smack*.

"What did you find out?" Karre reached between them and took hold of his shaft, intent on carrying out her own interrogation. She rubbed the tip along her folds.

Vidar closed his eyes. "Sorceress Magda plans to lead her minions against Spearhead. I've discovered her plot and alerted the king. He sends us reinforcements."

Karre hesitated at the news.

"Mm." He pulled her hips down, managing to get the tip of his cock inside her before she caught herself. "It will be a glorious battle."

Glorious? She hesitated again.

Vidar pulled her down on his cock and she

gasped as he filled her, stretching her sore muscles. "I will bring you much honor, my lady." He lifted her up. "You will find much pride in my sword." He jerked her onto his shaft.

Karre lost her train of thought. Vidar pushed his hand up between her breasts, urging her to lean back while on his cock. She braced her weight on her hands. The position put pressure along the sweet spot in her pussy. They thrust in a leisured rhythm and when her release washed over her it was perfect.

Vidar took her upper arm and pulled her to his chest. He groaned, stiffening as he came. He kept her impaled on him as he adjusted himself on the bed to lie down. He held her to his chest, rubbing along the small of her back.

"Perhaps it is too early to dine. We should stay right here," he whispered moments before his chest rose and fell in even breaths.

KARRE'S ARRIVAL at Spearhead couldn't have had worse timing. Apparently, they had gone decades without an attack on the fortress, but by Vidar's own words, a siege was imminent. She saw the evidence of his concern on the faces of the knights, in the way their rigid security became even more so. They drank less, brooded more and the number of guards patrolling the wall doubled.

Escape would not be easy, but how could she stay, knowing what she did?

"Who are you?"

Karre blinked, so lost in thought she didn't hear Vidar's approach. "What do you mean?"

Did Divinity say something to you?

In the last few days, cast under the rapturous spell of Vidar's touch, she had almost let herself forget that the corporation was out there. How could she think of evil deeds when his touch was so heavenly? An easy rapport developed, making for light-hearted banter but never serious conversation. It wasn't a perfect marriage, but it was the best relationship she'd ever been in. Well, to be honest, it was pretty much the only real relationship she'd ever been in.

If he tried to get serious, she'd distract him with sexual advances and invitations. His hand brushed her thigh under the table when they dined. His eyes met hers over the distance when he exercised with the men. He took her in their bedchambers, in hidden alcoves, in abandoned rooms, and once near the stables in a tight corner near the courtyard. He met her body's every demand, giving in to her whenever she wanted him, whenever she needed to stop his questions. But now, as he looked at her, she knew there was going to be no stopping the questions he'd been trying so hard to ask.

The passageway they stood in was unremarkable, other than the fact it had become Karre's sanctuary. With an old, locked door and dead end, only the maids came to the far end of the castle and not much at that. She'd already picked the old lock, only finding a dismal run of empty, old iron bar prison cells.

Her breath caught and she felt as if the surrounding castle closed in on her. Somehow, in the isolated almost primitive world of Staria, she'd managed to forget who she was. Maybe that's why she didn't try harder to leave. With so many knights, in the middle of nowhere on a low traffic plane, she had felt hidden, safe. Only after she learned of the Caniba had the urge to run filled her.

Karre glanced behind her, but it was the dead end. Vidar blocked her only escape. Her mind raced for her next move. "Is this a game? Did Sir Jacque give you more ideas?"

"It is a simple question," he said. "Who are you?"

Sandie, Faith, Temperance, Hope, Devil, Sparkle.

"I'm Karre." She forced a smile. "Your wife."

"Who were you before you came here?" he asked, leaning against the wall. He had an animalistic grace, even in his leisured pose.

Mazi, Ms. Lara Pentafore, Lady Pentafore, Madam Pentafore, Domma Pentafore.

"I was Karre." She widened her smile. "Not your wife."

Vidar didn't move for a moment, but then suddenly tilted his head back and laughed. "You once told me that there was an ocean on another plane and that you liked to stand on the cliffs so the water would splash on your face when the tides came in. Was that your homeland?"

"I also said that your skin reminded me of it." She reached to touch the side of his face, but he caught her wrist. "What is it?"

What did Divinity tell you?

"What are you hiding?" He didn't let go of her.

"Nothing." It took all her power to keep the innocent look on her face and she wasn't sure she was even successful. "There is nothing to tell."

Vidar studied Karre's blank expression. The king had ordered him to learn of his wife, but every time he tried, she distracted him with her amazing kisses and lush body. Now, as she artfully avoided his direct questions, he became concerned. Perhaps there was something she wasn't telling him. The faint hints he had were disconcerting—such as how she claimed to have been delivered against her will.

"I know you planned a trip," he stated. A maid had found her bag filled with trinkets from the fortress. All were things he'd freely give her, had she but asked. "Your bag had supplies for travel."

"You went through my room?" She frowned, narrowing her eyes as all pretense of the smile left her.

"Tell me why you chose to come here." He didn't let go and she didn't fight him.

"Who said I chose it? You picked me, remember?" She didn't move from her spot, didn't cringe or back away.

"Why will you not answer me? Who are you, Karre? One minute you're meek, the next bold. You never speak of your homeland or how you've come to be with me." It took all his willpower not to kiss her, not to let her tempt him with her perfect mouth and pleasing ways.

"I thought you said it was the gods who brought me here." She tried jerking her hand away. He kept her in his grasp, afraid she might run if he let go.

"Apparently, it's as simple as that. Perhaps you should ask them how I've come to be here, for I don't know the answer."

"Who are you?" Vidar yelled in frustration. His words echoed around them.

"I don't know anymore," she answered, just as loudly.

That surprised him. "You lost your memories?"

"No." Her pull on her wrist weakened as she stopped fighting his restraint. She studied his face, as if trying to decide her next words. "I-I scrambled my memories."

He tilted his head, studying her in confusion.

"But I still know which are mine. I know who I am. I just don't know *who* I am in the larger sense of the word. I've been..." She made a weak noise and shrugged, still not making any sense to him.

"You are my wife, Karre. I do not know if you understand fully what that means. Whatever it is you are running from cannot hurt you." Lifting his hand to her cheek, he ran his fingers along her jaw. "I will protect you."

Her gaze fell at his touch. "And what if you fall by the Caniba's hand? What then? Will you come back from the grave to protect me?"

"Then I will die with honor and make you proud."

"Proud?" Her eyes shot back up to meet his. "How is your death supposed to make me proud? I'm not a monster."

"The pride should come in my honor and in a good death."

"That brings me back to—how the hell are you supposed to protect me when you're dead?" She jerked her hand. He gripped harder until she stopped.

"Should that day come, another will take you under his protection." He hated to think it and refused to imagine her with another man.

"Passed to another husband? You mean I have to go back to the ceremony?"

"There are other ways. You could take..." He couldn't say it.

"Another husband while you're still around?" she finished astutely. "No, thanks, warrior. I think one is more than enough. I would hate to see the havoc two of you would wreak on my life."

He relaxed. Without realizing it, a knot had formed in his stomach. It now eased its hold, allowing him to breathe. "The Caniba will not harm you. Every man in Staria would give his life to make sure of it. I understand that you do not know our ways, but you are Starian now. We do not run from danger."

"All I do is run." She sighed. "Let go of my arm."

"Only if you promise to tell me how you came to be here."

"That's simple." She laughed, though the sound didn't hold any pleasure. Then, as if coming to a decision, she said, "I got caught and Divinity sent me here as my punishment."

"Caught? Doing what?" As promised, he let her go. She rubbed her wrist as she backed away from him. He widened his stance to block any retreat out of the dead-end hall.

Her mouth trembled before she answered, "Stealing documents from one of their safe houses."

Vidar's hand flexed. It was as if he could still feel her pressed into his palm. "A thief?"

"A very good thief," she corrected, "despite being caught."

He studied her face, waiting for her to smile, to laugh, to indicate she was joking. Instead, she merely looked at him, her expression guarded and closed. A thief? His wife?

"Honestly, my getting caught was dumb luck on Divinity's part."

"How so?"

Again she looked at him as if she decided whether or not she could trust him. "I knew the security risk was great, but how could I pass it up? It was a safe house."

"And?" he prompted.

"I went in smart. I met someone who brought me a briefcase full of security codes and a map. Getting in was easy. My only mistake was not having the right layout of the mansion. The architects forgot to mention the secret Divinity tech room behind the nursery mirror. Figures the one place I think to hide my wrist portal is on the door to a secret room. My misfortune and Divinity's dumb luck." She sighed, running her hands into her hair and shaking the locks. Muttering, she said, "I don't even know why we're talking about this."

He opened his mouth, but he didn't know how to answer. His wife was talking about infiltrating enemy territory. Such things were not easy or for the weak of heart. As if seeing her for the first time, he looked at her face, her cunning eyes.

"Sorry you pried? It's not the answer you were looking for, was it?" She walked past him, turning her shoulders so they didn't touch. "Too bad. It's the only answer I have." She made it around the corner before he could even think to stop her.

No, it wasn't the answer he looked for.

Karre hurried away from Vidar. What had she been thinking? Did she really expect him to react any differently? He tried to hide it, but she saw the disappointment in his eyes, the silent retreat of his emotions. She had tested him, not telling him anything Divinity didn't already know until she knew how he would react. Well, she'd gotten her answer. It was right there in his beautiful eyes.

Fool. Stupid idiot. I should have kept my mouth shut.

She didn't know where she was going, only that she had to keep moving, had to keep taking turn after turn, through endless passageways until she was sure to be lost—which was hard to do when she knew her way around. When she finally stopped moving, her hands shook and her knees wobbled, forcing her to the ground. She pushed into a small alcove, pressing her back to the hard stone as she drew her limbs into her chest. Her eyes stung and she realized that tears ran down her cheeks.

Stupid fool!

THE HALL WAS EERILY quiet as Karre made her way up to the head table to dine. The knights studied their meals, muttering in low tones that blended together to make one giant murmur of incoherent sounds. Nervously, she found Vidar. He'd sent a maid to command her to the hall to join the meal, which seemed strange since he'd not really spoken to her for the last couple of days. They didn't even share the same bed. She never thought she'd miss the feel of someone next to her as much as she did.

Karre's blue linen skirts felt abnormally heavy as she made her way to the head table. The darker blue of the corset pressed her stomach into her spine, but Jordinne had insisted on tightening it—something about bolstering the recently low morale of their leader. Maybe if she passed out from lack of air, Karre wouldn't have to see his questioning gaze.

"What has happened?" Karre asked, taking a seat by Vidar. His hand paused in the process of lifting a two-pronged fork to his mouth. "Is it the Caniba? Do they attack?"

"I wished for you to join us, as is your duty." He placed the meat into his mouth, chewing thoughtfully. "Your absence has been felt."

"Oh?" She watched his face.

"By the hall," he added. "The people have asked after you."

"Did you tell them?" Karre looked over the hall, to the rows of long tables filled with knights and their women. Several stared back at her. "About me?"

"I saw no need to announce it," he answered, frowning as he stabbed a vegetable with a little too much force. His words didn't really bring her any comfort.

"Then why is everyone so..." She paused, trying to think of the right word. "Tame?"

"Magda's scouts were killed near the border, not far from here. It is beginning." He didn't even try to shield her from it, not like before when she had to pry information out of him with her seduction.

"Are you leaving to fight?"

"Not yet, but soon. The king promises reinforcements. I'm to wait here for them to arrive prior to riding out to engage the sorceress before she and her armies pass into our borders." He didn't look at her as he continued to dine.

A maid brought her a trencher of food, causing Karre to jolt in surprise as it was set in front of her. She nodded her thanks and forced herself to eat, though in the end she rearranged the food more than consumed it. All her attention focused on Vidar. A cold chill worked over her from him. She hated him for it and hated herself for having told him even the smallest grain of truth. Lies always suited her purpose so much better.

"Have I made a long enough appearance?" Karre placed her fork on the trencher and reached for her goblet. The food might sit on her stomach like a rock, but the liquor would calm her nerves and hopefully numb her brain.

"If you're ready to go, I will escort you." Vidar took his goblet and finished off his drink.

"Why don't you just have the maids and knights trail me?" Karre muttered bitterly. "Or did you think I would not notice they have been keeping an eye on me the last couple of days?"

"You're paranoid."

"Uh-huh," she said dryly.

"The maids serve you and this castle. The knights are protection," he elaborated. "There is a threat nearby. I would think you liked the extra security. You seem to doubt my ability to protect you."

Feeling bitter, she let her hand brush up against the knife along her thigh and mumbled, "Don't worry about me. I will see to myself. Stay here in your hall."

Karre stood, wondering if he would follow her but unsure if she wanted him to.

Vidar waited until Karre disappeared through the arched doorway before standing to follow her. It had taken all he had not to go to her the last couple of days, but he needed time to process what she'd said. She admitted to being a thief. He resented her for it, even as he was drawn to her. A thief? Why had the gods tempted him with a thief? His family honor reeled at the injustice of it. What if the others discovered the truth? What if she left him, as she was surely going to do the night he came home from the marshlands?

Walking faster, he let his feet hit hard upon the floor. He shouldn't have to occupy his mind with Karre, not when there were more pressing matters of war. The people of Spearhead depended on him to protect them. The people of Staria needed him to maintain the borders. Magda was one of the most formidable foes they'd seen in a long time and she was planning an attack in his territory.

A woman is a woman, Vidar had told Oskar the day before his wedding. *The gods will give me what they give me. The king showed me the trade agreement. The women must be able to bear children, be in good health, able to do their duty and will know their place. What do I care if they are born in Staria, are brought through the fairy rings from distant lands or are traded for with Divinity aliens from another plane of existence? So long as she is not our enemy.*

Now he knew his mistake. Vidar should have demanded the king be more specific with his future, like the brides should not have a criminal past. Instead, all he could think about was finding a bride for sexual release, a soft, sweet body to slake his desires in. Karre did do that for him. His breathing deepened and his cock hardened until his pride warred with desire.

When he caught up to her, he wasn't sure if he would pleasure her or punish her. His hand wrapped around the back of her arm and he tugged her with him to the nearest door. With the hour being so late, no one occupied the sewing chamber. He let go of her and shut the door.

"Afraid I would run off?" She arched a brow, the sourness of her mood still apparent in her tone.

By all the bloody swords, she was still beautiful—even angry.

He didn't answer, at least not with words. Vidar grabbed the sides of her face and crushed his lips to hers. He needed to taste her, feel her. Her soft lips parted and he slid his tongue between them. In that moment, he didn't care what she had been before coming to him. Right now, she was his.

The pressures of his life faded, replaced by her mead-laden kiss. She moved against him, running her fingers into his hair, pulling him closer as if she needed him as badly as he needed her. What was it about this woman that made all logic fade?

He turned her, walking her past the large weaving loom toward the long sewing table. When the back of her thighs hit the tabletop, he kept kissing her, leaning her back until she was forced to crawl on top. Bolts of material cushioned her head as she stretched out before him like a feast of the flesh just waiting to be unraveled and eaten. Vidar fully intended to dine.

Karre moaned softly, wet with anticipation as he slowly undressed her—loosening her corset, pulling her garments over her head. No torches burned in the sewing chamber. Blue moonlight shone over them, streaming in from narrow windows to illuminate his face with an unearthly glow.

Vidar leaned over the table as he stood beside her, looking down at her naked form stretched out before him. He ran his hand over her breasts, brushing the nipples lightly so they peaked into hard buds. Not answering their aching call, he instead ran his hand along her ribs. She reached for him, but he pushed her arms away. Understanding his game, she lifted her arms over her head and didn't move.

Karre closed her eyes, following his playful touch with her mind, wondering at the change in him. It was as if he tried to learn her for the first time. The nerves tingled wherever he touched, sending out signals to her pussy until cream nearly dripped from her sex. Sensations skimmed along her toes, her calves, up her outer thighs and hips. He crossed her waist, circling her breasts before tracing the line of her arms. By small degrees his touch became firm as he retraced his original path, endlessly traveling over her body. By the time he made it back to her breasts and squeezed them in his palms, she was writhing on the hard wood.

She couldn't take waiting any longer and reached between her thighs to rub her swollen clit. It felt so good she cried out softly. Vidar took her breast in his mouth, aggressively sucking the nipple. His hand covered hers over her pussy. As she worked her clit, he slipped a thick finger into her slick sex and wiggled it around. Another of his fingers pressed down between the cleft of her ass, rubbing along the rosette of her anus. She rode their combined hands, sliding her finger into her pussy to join his. He went much deeper and the pressure of their fingers worked pleasurably against the sweet spot hidden inside her cavern.

Karre met with release, rewarding their efforts with a flood of cream. Breathing hard, Vidar crawled onto the table, drawing up between her thighs. Her ass rubbed against the hard wood as his weight held her hips down. He'd loosened his pants and now brought his thick, hard cock to claim his prize.

He thrust his hips forward, filling her to the brink. Wildly, he rode her, pounding and gliding in her wet pussy. Lighter tremors worked over her and she climaxed once more. Vidar grunted, suddenly stopping as he, too, found release.

Pinning her to the table with his weight, he pressed his nose to hers. Karre's legs fell along his sides. Their breathing mingled as he looked deep into her eyes. She waited for him to speak, but instead he pushed up and crawled off the table. Karre was slower to get up, sitting naked on the table as he dressed. When he finished, he turned to her and sighed heavily.

"Is this goodbye?" Her jaw tightened. Why else would he look at her like that?

"I had hoped you would come back to our chambers with me," he answered. "A bed would be much more comfortable."

Karre exhaled in relief. Giving him a small smile, she said, "Then hand me my gown. I have no wish to run naked through the halls."

8

Because right now, in this moment, Karre needed to confess everything, even if it was to a sleeping man.

For the first time since she had left her home world, Karre felt as if she might actually stop running. Sure, she knew the feeling might be fleeting, knew that tomorrow she might not be able to stop herself from going, but right now, as she looked at Vidar's sleeping face, she could actually imagine what it would be like to never jump to another plane. The idea terrified and exhilarated her because right now, in this moment, Karre needed to confess everything, even if it was to a sleeping man.

Karre sat on the bed, her legs crossed as she

leaned her elbows onto her knees. Her sated body should have forced her to sleep, but her racing mind refueled her with a nervous energy. If she decided to stay, then the Caniba would become her enemy. She would have to face the fear and learn to live with their constant threat. However, before that, she would have to convince Vidar that she should stay for something other than duty and the will of the gods. Maybe she even needed to convince herself. Or maybe there were gods watching them, moving people around at will because of some great, incomprehensible plan.

Confusion filled her, causing her thoughts to swim around in her head.

"I have been searching for a plane like this," Karre whispered, reaching to push a lock of hair off Vidar's forehead. "A low-tech place off the grid with very little inter-dimensional traffic. A person could disappear here. You have no idea how valuable that is. Divinity only wants your mineral water and perhaps to use you as a dumping ground for those they want to keep out of the main system—like me. They don't even have this world listed in their primary database. I have been thinking about that a lot. I memorized all four-hundred-thirty-six so-called known dimensions so I would know which ones to avoid and which to be careful on. Even that other prisoner bride at the ceremony said this place was uncharted. It means they don't have any use for it beyond what they're already trading. Once they have their fill of the water, they'll most likely never come back. I've seen it many times. With infinite worlds, they don't pay attention to all of them. They take what they can use and then they go."

He didn't answer, not that she expected him to as she watched his even breathing.

"It would be nice to have the PJP back. Um, that's the portable jump prototype that I had to travel to different planes without their main portal." She rubbed her wrist, thinking of the device. "You know, just to have it. Just in case I ever needed it." Karre laughed softly. "Just to get to my stash one last time to do what I need to."

Still, he slept.

"You should see some of the things I've collected. I have notes about missions Divinity wouldn't want anyone knowing about. I have pictures and video files and confessions. I have their office policies and contract copies that show obvious moral codes violations. I think that is why they want me alive, but where I can do no harm. They think by analyzing the PJP they will find out everywhere I have gone. What they don't know is that I have reset the history. They will never find what they're looking for."

She ran her hand lightly over his cheek and down his throat. His pulse beat steadily under her fingers. The fur blanket covered his stomach but left his chest bare. She drew her hand down to feel his heart beneath her fingers.

"Divinity is not the company you think it to be. They present themselves well, but they are not noble. They do things. Horrible things." She took a deep breath. "They make people do things, become things."

"What did they force you to do?"

Karre gasped, jumping back at Vidar's calm words. Apparently, he wasn't as asleep as she'd thought. How much had he heard? "You're awake."

His eyes opened, meeting hers. "Of course."

"You should have said something. You should have stopped me."

"Why would I interrupt? I was listening to you speak." He turned on his side, resting on his arm as he touched her naked thigh. "Please continue."

Karre hesitated. It was different now with him looking at her.

"Please," he insisted.

"Divinity's actions made me a thief. They

changed the entire course of my life." Karre pulled away from him, turning to stand on the floor. She felt too exposed as she strode naked to his trunk. Pulling up the lid, she grabbed the first tunic she found and pulled it over her head. "I've spent many years trying to prove what I know of the corporation, but they have covered their tracks very efficiently. I foolishly thought I might be able to stop them, but there are too many planes for them to hide."

"What is it you know?"

"That they stole lives. My land was called Grenlay Islah. I lived with my father near the water. He had retired from our country's military. I wanted to be a scientist and build better technology to be used in astronomical research. Astronomy is what we call the study of the universe beyond the earth's atmosphere—stars, sun, moon, planets. It seems so far away now, so small in importance to what I know now. My world isn't anywhere near close to discovering inter-dimensional travel. Normally such ideas were the thing of entertainment novels and holographic plays." Karre continued to pace, not meeting his eyes but very aware that they were on her. It seemed strange telling this story, perhaps because it was the truth. It had been a long time since she had told her truth to anyone.

"Come, my lady," he urged, patting the bed. "Sit. Please."

Karre refused, continuing to pace. "But you see, just because we weren't close to actually discovering parallel plane travel, it doesn't mean we didn't understand the concept. I think that's why Divinity came to us. We were primitive enough not to know how to chase after them but advanced enough to understand what had happened when they took us to a new plane."

"They stole your people?"

Karre stopped at his words and nodded, wondering if he could possibly believe her. No one else had. "Yes. Kidnapped them. Plucked them up and carted them away like they were picking flowers for their table. They took my father. They pulled him right off the street when he was out for a run. I would have never known what had happened, but I happened to be coming home at the time. I saw their uniforms, their alien equipment. No one would believe me. The police, um, enforcers of the law, thought I was distraught. They wanted me to seek medical help and have myself committed into a grief asylum. A few months later I saw the uniformed men again."

"What did you do?" he prompted when she paused.

"I followed them through their portal. It was like nothing I'd ever felt or seen. It's like being pulled apart on a molecular level and put back together. I thought I was dying. But then I showed up in their science facility. They were so arrogant, they didn't even have guards, like they knew no one could touch them or stop them. I grabbed one of their jackets, slipped it on and walked undetected through their facility. Someone asked me if I was from some place I had never heard of. I said yes. From there I integrated and learned, going from base to base, changing my appearance and my name until I found myself working for the science and technology department."

"And you sought the truth of what had happened?"

"There is no proof. I've looked. When the rest of the company, also known as those people not in charge, started to spread rumors about it, the executives terminated the project. That included permanently terminating those involved."

Vidar arched a brow.

"They killed everyone who knew anything," Karre clarified. "As for my father, I never saw him again."

"What did they take him for?"

"Gladiator fights," she said, "in some Romanesque plane. They took soldiers from my world and sold them to masters who forced them to fight to the death. The plane loved it because they felt all other planes were inferior to them. Other-worlders didn't have rights and were considered a subspecies."

"Were they at war? Not that such a thing would excuse forcing men from other worlds to fight a war that was not theirs to fight."

"No. It was for entertainment."

Vidar frowned in disgust. "To waste life for the sake of passing amusement. Shameful."

"When I finally got to the gladiator plane, I found my father's portrait painted on an arena wall." She paused, letting the pain of the memory roll through her. Karre had sat by that wall, weeping for hours, only leaving when one of the plane's residents came by trying to sell her loaves of green-tinted bread. "Apparently, he did really well before they decided to make him battle three wild beasts with his bare hands in celebration of their ruler's birth anniversary."

"I am sorry to hear this. My father died in battle, as well."

"At least it was a battle he chose to fight and not because some pompous rich master wanted to be entertained," Karre said, feeling bitter from the memory. "I might be a thief, but I only steal from Divinity and their allies for the purpose of stopping them."

"Why are you telling me this now?" Vidar frowned and pulled the fur covers from his hips to swing his legs around. Her eyes instantly turned to his waist before glancing away. "Do you think to leave me to continue your pursuits?"

"I had no intention of ever telling you any of this," she admitted with a humorless laugh. "I thought you were sleeping."

"Then I suppose it is good that I have been trained to sleep lightly." His hand shot forward and he grabbed her wrist. Gently, he pulled her toward him.

Karre resisted briefly but then gave up, needing to feel something other than pain and uncertainty. "I'm tired of running. I want to stay here, but I'm terrified of the Caniba. If I could just see them for myself, I'm sure I could put my mind at ease. The images of them that have been described to me are—"

"You have nothing to fear. We will protect you."

Vidar cupped her cheek, running his thumb over her lips. "I will protect you."

"I know better than anyone there are no guarantees in life. Rules and ideas that work on one plane do not on another. You can't promise that I will be safe. You can't promise that I will be protected. All you can do is promise you will do your best." Karre put her fingers over his lips to keep him from answering. "And all I ask is that you try."

His eyes narrowed, the intensity of the look all the more effective by the way the gold flecks picked up the firelight. "You have my word, my lady."

Karre was struck with the full impact of what she had revealed to him. More or less, it had been her life story. No one, not on any of the planes, knew so much about her.

She grabbed his face, pulling his lips to hers in a deep kiss. Moaning, she thrust her tongue between his lips. Vidar's hands roamed the backs of her thighs to push up the tunic she wore. He cupped her ass, rocking her hips forward.

Karre put her knee between his legs and crawled over him, urging him onto his back. When her lungs burned for need of air, she pulled back, panting as she looked down at him. This time there would be no games between them. She was too tired of pretending, of being someone else. "I don't want to run anymore."

Vidar pulled at the tunic shirt, helping her to lift it over her head. His hands skimmed over her breasts and ribs before settling on her hips. "You don't have to run. You are home."

Karre smiled. "But I do need to fight. If the Caniba are as bad as everyone says they are, then I wish to help in the battle to be rid of them. I can't sit here inside a fortress and do nothing. I need to focus on fighting so the fear doesn't overtake me. And if I could just get to my stash, I have things there that can help."

"There is no reason for you to go to battle." Vidar ran a lazy fingertip over her stomach, tracing the lines of her muscles. "Your presence in Spearhead helps greatly, my lady. Your beauty gives the men hope." He pushed his hips up, drawing attention to the ever-growing strength of his arousal.

She laughed, feeling giddy as she lightly scratched his chest. His cock brushed her stomach as she straddled his thighs. Karre kissed his neck, trailing her tongue over his flesh. His pulse beat against her lips.

Vidar wrapped his arms around her, caressing the small of her back and curve of her ass. Her breasts rubbed his chest until her nipples peaked against him. He moaned, his breath tickling her shoulder.

She laid her body fully to his, their legs twining, their flesh pressed together, hands exploring, hips rocking, moving in harmony. Parting her lips wide, she took in his breath as her mouth hovered over his. He flicked his tongue, enticing her to close the distance. She did, pouring all the passion she felt into her kiss.

Vidar groaned, rolling her onto her back. He shoved her thighs open with his, becoming more aggressive in his need. The tip of his cock brushed her folds, parting her with its firm persistence.

Karre closed her eyes and bit her lip. She arched her hips into him while pulling on his ass, silently begging him to take her. Every inch sang with pleasure and awareness. The mattress shifted with their weight, but he didn't thrust inside.

Breathing hard, she opened her eyes to study his face. He stared down at her, his narrowed eyes sweeping along her chest, up her neck to her lips. She worked her legs along his and reached between them to stroke his cock. A soft moan escaped him as she massaged the velvet length.

Muscles flexed and tensed along his chest as she

drew his cock along her moist folds, enticing and teasing at the same time. The thick tip bumped her clit. She jolted in pleasure and did it again.

Vidar entered her slowly, taking his time, letting her feel every sliding inch. She let go of his cock. Her hands explored everywhere she could reach. She wanted to touch all of him, taste all of him. When she drew him into her kiss, she moaned, sucking his tongue past the borders of her lips.

Karre angled her hips, meeting his thrust, urging him deeper into her pussy. A light sheen of sweat covered their bodies. She squirmed beneath him, her head rolling on the mattress as she broke their kiss to gasp for breath. Delightful sensations coursed through her body, radiating everywhere at once until she felt as if her body might explode into flames.

Vidar pushed up for leverage and he thrust harder, deeper. Her body tensed, her entire length going rigid as she met with release. The tremors racked over her. Vidar grunted, his hips jerking as he emptied himself into her. He collapsed against her, bracing his weight on his elbows to keep from crushing her.

After a long moment, he crawled off her. They readjusted on the bed and Karre burrowed under the covers, stretching out next to him. Suppressing a yawn, she said, "I really do want to help in the fight against the Caniba. If I am going to stay, I need to help. I have skills, ones that could be put to good use."

"Your desire to fight is understandable," he answered, closing his eyes and pulling her tight against him. "But your presence is enough. It gives us pride and a sense of duty to see what it is we are fighting for. A beautiful lady, a symbol of family and hope, is what you are to the warriors."

Karre's expression dropped some as she looked at him. He was serious. She stiffened in disbelief. "A pretty face to fight for?"

That wasn't exactly what she had in mind.

Vidar closed his eyes and nodded. "Yea. Very pretty."

"I'LL SHOW HIM PRETTY," Karre grumbled as she shoved the lock-picking pin into her upswept hair. The once-locked door swung open on silent hinges. She grinned, glancing down the long corridor to make sure she wasn't followed.

Karre had been into most of the rooms at Spearhead Fortress, but there were still a few locked doors she needed to get behind. The first one she'd visited that morning had been a weapons chamber, filled with rows of swords and shields, spiked maces and sharp daggers, spears and arrows. There had even been a few potion bottles and strange contraptions she had never seen before.

She shut the door behind her. Dust stirred as she walked. Unlike the rest of the fortress, the chamber had not been cleaned for some time. It made her search easier. She lifted her skirt, pulling it between her legs and tucking the end into the bottom of her corset so it wouldn't drag on the ground and give evidence of her being there. Stepping lightly, she placed her foot in the markings of larger footprints, following them across the room to a wall of shelves stuffed full of rolled parchments.

Karre pulled one from the shelf, noting its lack of dust. The wax seal had been broken and she unrolled it. The tight script was impossible to read. Although the words were probably ones she knew, apparently the Starian alphabet wasn't, because she couldn't read it. Without something to compare it to, it could take months for her to decipher what it said.

Putting the document back where she'd found it, she slowly retraced her steps to the door. She secured the room and straightened her gown before making her way down the corridor in search of the next locked door. Under her breath, she muttered, "I'll show him pretty."

Nothing. In the past, documents had always been one of the surefire ways of discovering fast information. Only, with no key to read the Starian language, she had no hope of learning anything from that method. She had searched every locked room in Spearhead and found no clue as to how she could help against the Caniba.

However, never one to give up, Karre decided to try the next best thing—gossipers.

"What are you mumbling about?" Jordinne asked, frowning as she looked up from her sewing. "Show him pretty?"

"I didn't say anything," Karre answered, grimacing.

"You've been saying it over and over." Bratene appeared more interested in poking her finger with the tip of her needle than applying it to her task. She didn't draw blood, but it seemed to alleviate her boredom. Then, mimicking, the woman said, "I'll show him pretty. How dare he say I'm just supposed to be pretty."

Jordinne laughed. "Got a taste of the Starian warrior, did you?"

"I got a giant bite of him," Karre grumbled, inciting laughter. Even Synna giggled from her place in the corner of the room.

"What did he do?" Jordinne cut her short thread and immediately began threading the needle with a new one. She worked fast, as if she'd sewn her whole life.

"He told me I was to be an inspiration for the warriors," Karre said. It seemed strange talking to the women, almost as if they were...friends. She hid her frown, uncomfortable with the word, unable to trust it completely.

"Ah, the 'something for the men to fight for' speech," Bratene said. "Methinks they want us to wear our best dresses every day."

"You mean our tightest corsets," Jordinne teased.

"They want us to scrub the floors and look like goddesses while doing it," Synna inserted.

"Well, to be fair, I like mine to be shirtless and silent." Bratene laughed. "And with a big sword to take into battle."

"Shameless," Synna murmured. "Utterly shameless."

Bratene threw a scrap of cloth at the woman. "I dare you to tell me you don't like a man with a big spear."

"I just like him to know how to wield it," Jordinne said, drawing Bratene's attention away from Synna. Karre noticed the woman tended to do that a lot, saving the more timid servant from Bratene's cruder barbs.

"I know you all said that we were supposed to let the men protect us, but who protects the men from themselves?" Karre studied them carefully.

"Every woman knows a man cannot take care of himself," Synna answered, reaching toward Jordinne to grab a small knife to cut her thread. "If not for women, they'd be running about naked and covered in dirt."

"Starving," Jordinne inserted.

"Stinking," Bratene added.

"And, according to Vidar, with nothing to fight for," Karre mused.

"Women bring civility to men." Synna had managed to rethread her needle and continued to sew.

"They need it with Sorceress Magda so close. We

have never seen such a formidable foe in my lifetime, or my mother's." Jordinne put her work down and stretched her arms over her head. "I will gladly celebrate the day she is no more."

"I think I can get to Magda," Karre announced, her hand shaking. Bratene and Jordinne gasped in unison and Synna dropped her sewing on the floor. When no one spoke, she continued, "I've been listening to the men, hearing their stories of how she comes up from the ground. So, it can be concluded that they live in caves. I have a skill for blending in. It will be easier if I can get my equipment from off-world, but if you all—"

"No," Jordinne shook her head, interrupting. "Vidar would never allow it. The men would never allow it."

"We will never allow it." Synna slowly reached to the floor to pick up her sewing.

"Just consider for a moment," Karre said. "I've been to some of the most advanced planes in the parallel universes and to some of the most primitive. I don't want to live in fear of Magda and I don't want to risk..." Karre paused.

I don't want to risk losing my husband, my new life, to some crazy cannibal queen. I don't want to be taken by another husband should Vidar fall in battle.

A sharp pain radiated in her chest and she pressed her hand between her breasts to try to stop it.

"We don't doubt your skills, my lady, but—" Synna began, her tone placating.

"Then help me," Karre pleaded. "Tell me everything you know about her encampment. Surely your men talk. If I can go there, if I can gain some kind of intelligence that will help us conquer—"

"And what if you are captured? What happens to Vidar when he loses a wife who has left him without children?" Synna demanded.

Karre eyed the woman, surprised at the passion in her normally mild voice. "I haven't given children much thought."

What else could she say? Children? She had barely given herself time to adjust to the idea of not running away, of staying as a wife.

"Well, perhaps you should give it thought," Synna quipped.

"Children here? With Magda at our door?" Karre studied her hands, twining and untwining her fingers. Come to think of it, she hadn't seen too many children around the fortress.

"What would you have us do?" Jordinne inquired. "March alongside the men into battle? Wield a sword and pray for an honorable death?"

"I have no wish to fight in battle," Bratene said. "I am content with my place."

"Neither do I," Karre admitted. "I'm not talking about fighting in combat. But if I could find how Divinity brought the other brides here, I know I could find a way to help. I could gather information. I could tell the knights where to find the sorceress."

The women stared at her, their expressions blank.

"You don't know where the Divinity portal is, do you?" Karre sighed. If she could get to her stash, she would have a better chance of infiltrating the sorceress' encampment. "It's not in my nature to do nothing."

"Here," Synna thrust a piece of cloth at her. "Busy your hands. Then you will be doing something."

9

*Because right now, in this moment, Karre had no idea
who she was supposed to be.*

Strategizing and talking and thinking about
fighting the Caniba sorceress was a lot different than
actually finding the means to implement her plan.
Since Karre's father had been abducted, she'd run
toward danger, faced unknown planes, traveled to
other dimensions until there were times she could
barely remember her own name, let alone her own
land. She had learned how to set aside her fears, and
facing a Caniba queen, once she'd decided to do so,
wasn't something she would back away from. When
Karre invented a role, she became that person—the

maid, the dancer, the noblewoman, the pedestrian, the baker. Whatever the job called for, that was who she was—with or without the damned memory implanter.

But now? What role was Lady Karre, wife of Sir Vidar of Spearhead?

She hadn't lied to Vidar when she said she didn't want to run anymore. At that moment, it had been the truth. As she looked at his firelight-caressed face, she had wanted to sit on that bed forever, staring at him, breathing him in. However, now as she looked over the main hall filled with knights, hearing the coarse banter as she sat alone at the head table, she wasn't so sure she wanted this to be her everyday normal. Because right now, in this moment, Karre had no idea who she was supposed to be.

Vidar had sent word that he rode out with some of the men. A strange feeling overwhelmed her, but she couldn't figure out what it was. Apathy? Regret? Frustration? Confusion? Resolution? Desperation? Enclosure?

How could she wait and do nothing? The maids refused to discuss any further plan of action. So was this it? Was this her life? Would she sit at her throne-like place above the main hall, staring out at the many knightly faces, watching them eat, hearing them talk, worrying about the Caniba? Day after day?

"Worrying about Vidar?" she whispered, frowning into her lap. No one heard the soft question and she was left without an answer.

How had she become so invested? How could she let her guard slip? How had he wormed his way into her emotions?

Karre found it hard to breathe and reached to grab the stout liquor. She gulped it down, feeling it burn its way to her stomach. Then, as realization dawned on her, she choked, coughing it back up so that it sprayed over her trencher of food, onto the table and floor.

"My lady?" Jordinne's voice penetrated the fog that settled over Karre's senses. The hall became quiet, or perhaps she couldn't hear it over the heavy beat of her heart. A hand pulled at her sleeve, forcing her around. Jordinne stared at her in concern. "My lady?"

"I think I love my husband," Karre whispered, unable to work her mind out of the daze. She pulled her arm from Jordinne's hold and stumbled away from the table.

"Karre?" Vidar's heart hammered in his chest as he rushed toward her bedchamber. "My lady, are you well? What's happened? Karre, are you in here?"

Strange reports of her stumbling from the main hall had been carried to him on his way to scout the marshlands. Jordinne assured him that his wife had not been poisoned, but after riding hard to get to her, he had to see her for himself. An unseen hand squeezed his heart in his chest at the thought of losing her. He didn't care to analyze the feeling too closely.

As he walked into her bedchamber, he noted, not for the first time, the décor Karre had added to the room. It looked like nothing he had ever seen. The warrior in him wanted to retreat, away from the lush environment into the familiar world of stone and steel. The man in him wanted to lie on the bed and let the thoughts slip from his mind as his wife attended him in lavish comfort.

Seeing her resting on the bed, he slowed. Karre lay on her stomach, her back rising in even breaths as she slept. Her face was turned to him, shadowed by the way her shoulder blocked the firelight. He smiled, his eyes moving down over her naked back. Silken covers molded over her ass and hips, outlining the shape of her legs.

He leaned against the bed and brushed her hair from her face. Then, not wanting to disturb such a beautiful sight, he made a move to leave. Karre grabbed his wrist, stopping him from turning away. She opened her sleepy eyes, blinking heavily.

"You're not the only light sleeper." Her words were thick and a little husky. "I thought you had to leave."

Reaching for her, he touched her forehead, feeling it for heat. "I got word that you were ill."

"Ill?" She didn't move from her stomach. "No. Not ill."

"Then?"

"Just tired." As if to prove her point, she stifled a yawn and straightened in a stiff stretch. "Has something happened? Why are you back?"

"Are you so eager to see me gone?" A small smile curled on his lips as he teased her.

"I'm glad to see you safe." Finally she turned, keeping her body hidden beneath the covers as she lay on her side.

The smile turned into a wide grin. "I am glad to see you well."

"I'm glad to see you here." She reached for his tunic, pulling him toward her. Her eyes fixed on his lips as she brought him into her kiss. Warmth radiated from her sleep-flushed skin. She kept the kiss brief, only slightly parting her lips.

"I am glad to see you naked." He chuckled softly and slid his hand over her covered hip. Her lashes dipped low over her eyes, shading them. Her breathing deepened. "And I am glad to hear that you have grown feelings for me."

She stiffened under his hand. "W-what? Who, ah, where did you get that impression? I didn't say... What?"

"Is it not true? Did you not say you loved me?"

"Jordinne," she whispered in realization. "She heard me." She grimaced slightly. "She told you."

He'd not dared to fully believe the maid's words until that moment, when he saw the uncertainty in her eyes. A strange feeling unfurled in his chest, warm, new, uncertain. Everything about his training as a warrior spoke against such feelings. Men had to be hard and in complete control. Friendship was expected in a marriage. Caring was encouraged. But love? How did he even know what that meant? How would he even know if he felt it? The idea was as foreign as peace. Sure, they knew about the concept but never expected to see it implemented in their lifetimes.

"Yes," she whispered, her breathing deepening.

"I have grown feelings for you."

The words pleased him. How could they not? Strange emotions filtered through him but he wasn't equipped to decipher their meaning. He needed more time to think and analyze. He refused to lie to her. He respected her too much for that. "You are a fine wife, my lady."

Karre's lashes lowered over her eyes and for a moment she didn't move. Then, giving him a small smile, she said, "Come to bed. It's late."

"Yea." He kissed her temple. "Let me hang my weapons. I'll be back in a moment."

You are a fine wife, my lady.

Karre watched Vidar leave, forcing all emotions from her expression. When he disappeared out of the door, she turned in the bed and faced the wall. A fine wife? She told him about her feelings and he called her a fine wife? She wasn't sure if she should cry or punch him in the nose. No one liked their feelings to go unrequited, but she couldn't force him to love her.

But a fine wife? Fine? Surely he could have managed a much better compliment. Then again, he was Starian. It was quite possible he couldn't manage a better compliment.

She took a shaky breath and then another, trying

to exhale the pain building in her chest. Closing her eyes, she focused on keeping her breathing even, pretending to sleep. Vidar came back into the room. She heard him moving behind her, the whisper of his clothes as he undressed, the stirring of the fire as he tended the flames.

The mattress moved under his weight as he climbed into bed. She rocked gently before he settled next to her. His hand slid along her hip before coming to rest. He merely held her, didn't try to wake her with kisses or insistent desires. Within moments, he slept. Karre opened her eyes to peek at him. He lay naked beside her, as perfect in form as any finely carved statue. Her heart pounded, as if begging him to wake up and look at her, to say something other than she made a fine wife. He didn't stir and she knew deep sleep would not find her again that night.

LIGHT FILTERED through the narrow slit, casting the bedchamber in a sleepy light. Karre yawned, not feeling rested. She adjusted her limbs on the bed, stretching along Vidar's side. Her movement roused him and he blinked heavily, suppressing a yawn.

"Good morn, lady wife," he said, instantly

pulling her close. His arms felt so good and protective. For a moment she forgot why her heart ached so badly. "I much prefer waking up next to you than surrounded by soldiers in the marsh encampment. You are much prettier." He paused, brushing his lips against her temple. "And you smell better, much sweeter."

Surprised at the gentleness in him, she waited to see what he would do next.

"You do not speak." Vidar placed his knuckle under her chin and turned her face toward his. "Did you not rest well? I tried not to disturb you."

"Mm," she moaned softly, snuggling closer to him. "It's too early to speak."

He glanced at the window. "But it is daylight."

"Early daylight," she corrected.

"I am not tired." His hand glided down her back, pressing her stomach against his. Since they'd slept naked, there was nothing to hinder their meeting flesh. The unmistakable interest of his arousal formed along her hip. His voice lowered into a husky murmur. "And yet I cannot seem to force myself out of bed to tend the morn exercise."

"Exercise," she purred, running her hand up his chest. Everything about him stirred her passions—his look, his feel, his smell. She detected the whisper of his breath against her cheek, tickling her flesh. His eyes pierced her with their intensity. The exhaustion drained from her limbs, replaced by the restless energy of desire.

Vidar kissed her briefly before drawing his mouth along her jaw to her neck. She wanted him so badly, always wanted him. Strong hands ran along her body, along her hip to the outside of her thigh. Fingers skated over her knee before finding the path between her legs that would lead them to her center heat. Her sex welcomed his touch with a flood of cream.

His lips moved over the heavy pulse in her neck. Taking his time, he pressed measured kisses along her collarbone to her shoulder. He angled her onto her back to give his mouth better access to her breasts. A tremble worked over her needy flesh. Every nerve focused on where they touched. Soft noises left her, joining his longer moans.

Vidar wrapped his lips around a taut nipple, sucking gently. He massaged the other breast, mimicking the movements of his circling tongue with his fingers. Karre caressed everywhere she could reach, following the defined contours of his muscles. Sensations overwhelmed her, drowning out all thoughts.

When he came above her, parting her legs with his, his mouth joined her once more. This time the kiss deepened until their tongues waged a war in their mouths. With the intensity of pleasure exploding between them, they both were equally victorious. Her lungs burned for air and she had to pull away. Lips parted, she panted against his mouth.

Vidar brought his body to hers. The tease of his cock slid over her pussy, pressing into the wet hold of her slit. There was a gentleness in him that she hadn't seen before as he delved forward, filling her with his strength. They rocked together in perfect unison, breathing each other in with every thrust.

His eyes held hers in their grasp as effectively as his body pinned her to the bed. Tension built, so sweet and pure it made her heart ache with the intensity of its promise. As her body climaxed, racked with pleasure, she wished she could hold on to the moment and never let it go.

Vidar jerked, stopping movement as he came inside her. Grinning, he rolled to his side. His arms fell limp in complete relaxation. "A man could die happily in your arms, my lady."

It wasn't "I love you" but she decided it would do for now. Smiling sleepily, she answered, "Death is not something I'd ask of you, Sir Vidar."

VIDAR COULDN'T STOP GRINNING as he sauntered through the courtyard. Everything seemed more pleasing than normal—the sky was a wonderful shade of blue, the air was sweet, exercise enjoyable, his fortress proud and strong, his people smiling despite the threat lurking at their gate. He couldn't name what it was that had changed. Maybe the sun shone with a different light. Maybe the cook used a new herb in the porridge and it altered his perspective. Or maybe it had something to do with the invisible thread he felt connecting him to his wife.

Invisible thread? It made no logical sense and yet there the thought was.

He passed through the fortress entrance into the hall. Servants wiped the empty tabletops, finishing up their cleaning of the morn meal.

"Sir Vidar, I must speak with you."

Vidar stopped walking as he heard his name. Seeing the maid Synna approaching him, he nodded at her, encouraging her to speak.

"It is about Lady Karre," the servant said.

His smile faltered. He glanced around. Everyone else was far enough away the conversation wouldn't be overheard. "What about my lady?"

Synna opened her mouth and hesitated, as if rethinking her decision to come to him. "You know what happened to Sir Fredrick after he infiltrated Magda's camp."

"He is a hero," Vidar placed a steady hand on her arm. "He was very brave to try. None doubt that."

The woman glanced to the floor. "He is locked away in a room lined with mattresses to keep him from bashing his own skull against the stone walls, forever changed by what that witch did to him. I would not see your wife face the same hero's fate."

"My wife?" Vidar stiffened, feeling as if he'd been kicked. He pushed Synna aside, ready to surge past her. "Has she been taken?"

"Hold." Synna grabbed his wrist before he could run out of the fortress. "She is yet unharmed. I believe she still sleeps. But I feel I must warn you of what she plans. It is my duty."

Vidar crossed his arms over his chest. The pleasure of his day drained into a hard knot of stress in his stomach.

"She thinks she can get to the sorceress by infiltrating the Caniba's world." Synna grabbed his crossed arms and squeezed so hard her nails dug into his flesh. He barely noticed the sting it caused. "Please, Sir Vidar, stop her. Do not let her face the madness. Do not let her end up like my husband. Death is better than such insanity."

He sighed, trying to calm the woman even as he fought the urge to run to Karre and demand she give up such foolish thoughts. "I would never allow it, Synna. Thank you for coming to me, but I swear Lady Karre is not going to face the Caniba."

"You ARE NOT to leave the fortress without supervision."

Karre looked at her bedchamber door in surprise, unable to believe her ears. She had heard Vidar come into his room but hadn't expected him to barge through her door making stern demands before she even managed to get out a greeting. Endeavoring to remain calm, she asked, "And why not?"

"I know of your plan to face the Caniba queen. I forbid you from leaving this fortress without my permission." Vidar breathed so hard his shoulders lifted with each breath, giving him the air of a predatory beast who had just run down his prey.

Karre pulled the laces of her blue corset bodice tight and tied them with a slipknot to hold them in place. She smoothed the long skirts of the cream-colored underdress while keeping a steady eye on him. "I see."

"Then it is settled." The stiffness of his shoulders began to relax.

Instead of agreeing, she said, "I have traveled to some of the most advanced planes in all of the parallel universes and I have been to some of the most primitive. I have been put into situations you cannot imagine, tortured, chased—"

"That has nothing—" he began.

"Sought after," she continued, raising her voice to drown out his. "I'm not some weak, delicate flower that you have to water and protect. I know you do not want to hear it, but you can't plant me in the ground and tell me to look pretty and not to move. I have thorns and—"

"Are saying you want to farm?" His arched a brow.

"I'm saying that you cannot tell me what to do. I stay because I want to stay, not because anyone told me to." A dull ache started in her chest at his arrogant expression. "You said you had prisoners. If I can get to the Divinity portal, I can get this device that will help me read the prisoners' minds. I can get to Magda. I can—"

"I will not listen to this."

"I'm the perfect spy with my talent and skills," she yelled louder. "The way you all protect women around here no one would ever suspect me. Your problem is that you sent in warriors when you should have sent in someone more subtle. Just consider—"

"No." The denial was flat, hard.

"Then consider your people and how stopping Magda would save many lives. I've seen the men present the sword of the fallen knights to their wives. Those women might nod and accept the death token, but I see their eyes. Something dies inside of them." Realizing she screamed, she took a deep breath and eased her tone. "I do not want to be presented your sword."

"Karre." Her name came out on a sigh as he closed his eyes and ran his hands through his hair.

"What of children? I know you want them, but you can't want them to grow up with Magda. All I'm saying is I'll go in, find out where she's hiding and I'll get out. I'll report the layout. I'll—"

"No."

"You can't stop me. If you don't tell me how to get to the Divinity portal, I'll go on my own."

"Do not test me," he warned. "Give me your word of honor that you will forget this foolish plan."

Karre bristled at his decree, not liking this demanding side of him. Anger bubbled inside her, flooding every nerve. "If you want to keep me here, you're going to have to tie me up in the courtyard and put me under guard because that is the only way you're going to make me do what you want me to."

With that, she marched toward the bedchamber door, storming out on her husband, intent on getting away from him.

"Karre!" he yelled, chasing after her. "I have not finished discussing this."

Thinking more of defying him than what they fought over, Karre ran, going faster as he followed behind her. Words flew between them, growing in heat and intensity. By the time they reached the main hall, they were yelling at the top of their lungs, making a spectacle. "Leave me alone!"

"You will do what I say," he demanded.

"I will not have you dictate orders to me," she returned. Those gathered in the hall turned to watch the argument. "I am not yours to command."

Vidar stiffened and she knew he was acutely aware of their audience. "I am your husband. I have every right to command."

Karre didn't care who heard them. To her thinking, it was best everyone knew her position. Refusing to back down, she balled her fists. "Oh, yeah? And you think you're man enough to make me?"

10

Because right now, in this moment, she was tied up
and put under guard.

Shadows fell heavy over the wide courtyard, cooling the heat of the day as a gentle breeze swept over the open yard. Women carted buckets of water from the well into the fortress. They did their best not to look at Karre, but she saw them peeking from the corner of their eyes. She couldn't blame them, because right now, in this moment, she was tied up and put under guard.

Damn him.

Karre grimaced, thinking of Vidar as she stood,

tied to a T-shaped post, in the middle of the court-yard. A chain ran along the top, binding her wrists over her head and a large shackle held her waist to the post, leaving her feet free to kick at the dirt. Her ties didn't hurt, merely annoyed.

Somehow their argument had spiraled out of control and she'd ended up in the courtyard by her own taunting. The anger felt good, the release, the passion, the heavy breathing. Still, how could she back down? She wasn't his to command, not like that. If he could protect *her*, then she could return the favor and protect *him*. She loved him, but she wouldn't be controlled by him.

"Way to take a stand," she mumbled, more bored than annoyed. "I could have told him to lock me in my chamber. Or chain me to the head table with a bottle of liquor."

Karre kicked at the ground with her toes, trying to find someone, anyone, who would look directly at her so she could call them over to keep her company. Maybe she could convince them to let her go. It could be a diverting game—making Vidar catch her. The idea caused her body to tingle and her mind to swirl with deliciously wicked thoughts.

"Focus, Karre," she admonished, pushing aside all sexual desires. This was bigger than a mere sexual game. This was her life, her future. She needed to concentrate.

"Have you reconsidered?"

Karre struggled to turn. Vidar's voice came from behind her. She wondered how long he'd been standing there. With the breeze hitting her face, she hadn't detected him. When she couldn't see more than the side of his arm, she said, "Have you?"

"I have no wish to leave you out here, but you challenged my authority in the great hall in front of my men." The heat of his breath brushed over the back of her neck as he leaned close. "Simply promise me you won't try to spy on the Caniba and we can end this. I only seek to keep you safe."

"I don't know. I'm rather comfortable right here." She lightly swung her hands back and forth, taking what little movement she could. "It's a beautiful day."

"You are a frustrating—*grrr*." With that growl, he marched off. His steps stopped and he came back. Very softly, he said, "If you change your mind or become uncomfortable, signal the knight on the battlement. Just say the word and we can forget this... *misunderstanding*. I have no wish to keep you prisoner like this. Please, my lady."

"Do you reconsider? Because the way I see it, if

you can protect me, I can try to protect you. I will not make you a promise I do not intend to keep. I may be many things, Vidar, but I will not lie to you."

"I cannot reconsider."

"Then, I'm sorry, but I'm quite comfortable remaining right here," she answered.

"As my lady wishes." He touched her hip before leaving once more.

Her mind focused on her hip where he'd touched her. Sexual thoughts tried to invade, taking over her reason, trying to make the whole captive scenario a game. Arousal warred with logic and for a moment she let arousal win. Her breathing deepened, causing her bodice to feel tight against her breasts. She closed her eyes, imagining Vidar dressed all in black, stalking around her as if ready to pounce—potent, sexual, animalistic...

The creaking of the front gate snapped her out of her budding fantasy. She tensed, watching to see who came through. Was it more soldiers carrying the blades of the fallen to new widows? Even knowing Vidar wouldn't be among them, she felt her stomach tighten at the mere thought of it.

I cannot back down.

First knights entered, filing in two by two. She

searched them for fresh wounds but didn't see any. Synna and Jordinne hauled baskets heaped with laundry, pausing to watch the visitors. Synna glanced at Karre, looking incredibly guilty. Karre sighed. So that was how Vidar discovered her plan. She should have known. Synna had tried a couple times to point out how foolish Karre's words were.

As a man entered, clearly the leader if not by his carriage then definitely by his massive size, she narrowed her gaze in recognition. He was one of the bridegrooms from the ceremony at Battlewar. What was his name? Lord Big Moody Knight?

Behind the large knight, horses pulled a cart. Seeing the blonde bride who had been a part of the marriage ceremony, Karre forced her expression to go blank. Spearhead guards pushed the oversized doors of the main gate closed and latched them with a thick timber.

The cart stopped and the blonde emerged, rubbing her back and wobbling on shaky legs. Wondering what, if anything, the woman had learned, Karre whistled loudly and yelled, "I see you've survived." Then, before she could stop herself, she added, "I had my doubts."

Karre cringed inwardly as the blonde jerked in

MICHELLE M. PILLOW

surprise and looked over. The comment was true, but she hadn't meant to say it. The blonde seemed weaker than the others and not at all suited to handling the giant man who had claimed her.

Lilith. The name hit her, crawling out of her memory. *Her name is Lilith. He is Lord Sorin of Firewall.*

Karre smiled, wiggling her fingers in greeting. Her chains jingled at the movement. Hurrying on before Lilith could think about her last comment, Karre said conversationally, "Great weather we're having."

Lilith glanced around the yard. Sorin stood near his dirt-covered knights and equally caked horses. With her husband occupied, Lilith cautiously walked to where Karre waited. Under her breath, she asked, "Karre? Are you all right? What's happened here?"

"Small misunderstanding," Karre answered with a short, dismissing laugh. "Nothing to be concerned about. How's your guy been treating you?" Karre leaned to the side and pretended to study the newcomers. "Which one was he again? The big guy?"

"I found the way out." Lilith whispered urgently. Karre's easy smile dropped and her eyes narrowed at the information. Maybe Lilith wasn't as weak as she had first thought. "It's at Battlewar Castle in the dungeons. I tried to leave to bring back help, but it's too guarded."

Karre didn't answer. Her mind raced. Battlewar? She was sure she could find her way back there, but how would she make it undetected? Even if she managed to get past the guarded gate and through Battlewar Village unnoticed, she would have to face the crowd of knights who roamed the castle. The place was a palace compared to Spearhead Fortress in both size and population.

Lilith continued, "Have you seen Jayne or Paige?"

Karre's smile lifted with great effort, though her mind stayed focused on the conversation. "No. You're the first."

"I promised Jayne I'd try to get word to everyone." Lilith bit her lip, checking to make sure they weren't overheard.

Young boys who worked in the stables led the horses away. Servants welcomed the men, ushering them inside. Friends greeted friends.

"I'll draw you a map and write down the code to my home dimension." As Lilith spoke, Lord Sorin turned his attention to them. "I'll find a way to get it to you, just check your chambers. Someone at

Divinity headquarters should help anyone who comes through the portal if you tell them what happened."

Yeah, right. Divinity would just love to help me escape them. Thanks for the offer, but I think I'll pass.

"If you see Jay—" Lilith continued.

"Sh." Karre shushed the woman. Sorin was too close. To cover what Lilith had revealed, she announced, "Yep, beautiful weather for a ride into battle."

"My lady," Sorin said, joining them. He nodded at Karre, as if acknowledging her statement as fact.

"My lord." Karre bowed her head, the action not as respectful when done with rattling chains. Lilith opened her mouth to speak, as if to reassure Karre in her tied up state. Karre could care less about her ties. She wasn't scared of Vidar hurting her. To cut off any sentiment, Karre began to hum playfully as if she hadn't a care in all the dimensional planes.

Sorin led his wife away. Karre watched the knee-length flaps of his black long tunic hit purpose-fully against his legs. Lilith stumbled next to him, causing the big warrior to stop. Curious, Karre stared as he gently placed his finger beneath Lilith's chin and lifted her eyes to look at him. Though she strained, she couldn't hear their words. Sorin's motions were gentle when he finally led Lilith away.

"Hm. It would seem she has tamed her beast," Karre said to herself, somewhat impressed. "Now, if only I could win this battle with mine."

Aggravating wench!

Vidar paced his chambers, hating that Karre was tied up in the courtyard, hating that he'd ordered it done to her, hating that she had publically goaded him to do just that. And for what? Because he had laughed at the incredibly ridiculous idea of his wife infiltrating an evil sorceress' lair as a spy? Okay, so he could have held his temper in the great hall, but she'd been yelling too.

Contrary to her obvious lack of faith in his ability to protect her, he did have a plan. Already his men informed him Lord Sorin was close, just as the king promised. Once reinforcements arrived, they would handle Magda and her followers.

"Sir Vidar," a maid said from the door. "Lord Sorin has arrived."

"Thank you, Calla." Vidar tugged his tunic over his head, tossed it on the bed and grabbed a fresh one from his trunk before heading toward the main hall to greet his guest. Pulling it over his head as he walked, he let the long sides of the black tunic fall around his knees.

His guests were seating themselves at the head table when he arrived. Lady Lilith clutched her husband's arm and Vidar heard her whisper, "What's happening to Karre? Why is she tied up?"

Vidar frowned. His fellow Starians would never question such a thing. It wasn't her concern, but the business of a man and his wife. Had Karre actually been abused, the people of Spearhead would have revolted against their leader in protest. To stop further questioning in wake of graver concerns, he answered before Sorin could, simply stating, "A misunderstanding."

"Oh," Lilith made a soft noise and had the decency to glance away.

Vidar bowed toward Sorin, acknowledging him before doing the same to Lilith. The lady had an angelic face and the coloring to match. Vidar much preferred his darker temptress.

Aggravating seductress!

"Lady Lilith, may I introduce Sir Vidar," Sorin said. "This is his home."

"Only until the king assigns it to another," Vidar

answered politely. He tried not to think of Karre, even as he glanced over the hall in hopes that one of his men came to inform him of her contrition. "My lord, if you would come with me?"

He didn't wait for a response as he made his way to the old scroll room. Reaching to his waist, he pulled at a small pouch near his knife to take out a key. Because of the nature of the documents stored inside, the chamber had not been cleaned for a few years. Ignoring the dust, he strode across the room to a wall of shelves filled with rolled parchments.

"What news?" Sorin inquired, shutting the door behind him.

"Sorceress Magda has yet to show herself, but they found tracks near the marshes and we uncovered plans too. I've sent word to the marshes that we ride at dawn to join them." Vidar unrolled a map of the land surrounding Spearhead Fortress and laid it on the table, holding it open. "Lady Lilith is welcome to stay here. Her every comfort will be met and I will leave a small contingency of soldiers to guard the fortress."

Even though Sorin was higher ranking by birth, Spearhead Fortress was entrusted to Vidar, as was the nearby borderlands. These were his decisions to make and Sorin did not dispute them. Once on the battlefield, they would each lead their own armies.

Sorin nodded. "I agree. It is not safe at the encampment and my lady is delicate to the ways of war. She will remain here."

Vidar thought of his wife. She was far from delicate. "Lady Karre wishes to join the war."

"These women they send us." Sorin chuckled, clearly thinking Vidar jested. Leaning over the map, he asked, "Where is your army positioned? I will send orders to my men. By the grace of the gods, we'll have Magda's head."

KARRE GRINNED as the lock binding her wrists opened with a soft click. It hadn't been easy in her position, but she managed to get the lock-picking tool untangled from her hair. She found she much enjoyed the challenge, freeing herself in a courtyard filled with Starian knights. Clearly they underestimated her. Even her guards kept a lax eye on her as they talked with the newly arrived guests. Though, to be fair, since Vidar told her he didn't want to keep her prisoner, they probably weren't too concerned with making sure she stayed bound. And really, if she got caught, it's not as if anything would happen.

As the courtyard quieted and guests filtered in for the eve meal, Karre slipped out of her ties and made her way through the back passageways to her bedchamber. Her muscles were a bit sore, but she didn't mind. She found herself smiling as she thought of the look that would cross over Vidar's face when he discovered she had escaped. That image led to others—him running after her, barging into her chambers, finding her on the bed, the captor after his naughty captive.

Ugh! *Quiet, brain,* Karre scolded her wayward thoughts. *This isn't a game. It's not about sex. I'm making a point. He needs to know he can trust me. He needs to know I can take care of myself.*

Seeing a basin of water, she slowly bathed, running a wet cloth over her flesh. The fire dried her as she paced naked through her chamber, stretching her muscles and restlessly plotting. How to get to Battlewar to the portal? Or would her "daring" escape from the courtyard be enough to convince Vidar that she knew what she was doing?

She stopped. A chill crept up her spine, filling her with dread. Karre slowly turned.

"I knew that locator we implanted would come in

handy." Director Tomes lounged against the wall as if he'd always been there, watching, waiting. The tight black of his Divinity uniform molded to his body like a second skin and the wrist portal wrapped his wrist. He was alone. His cold eyes dipped over her naked body and he smiled. "You're looking well."

Karre fought the urge to run and hide. Forcing her limbs to remain steady, she went to her trunk to pull out her most conservative tunic.

"There is no need to cover up for me. In fact, Sparkles," he paused and arched a brow. "May I call you Sparkles?" When she didn't answer, he continued, "Why don't you put the gown on the bed?"

Karre made a move to pull it over her head.

"I insist." He tapped a laser pistol as it rested in a side holster next to his leg.

Karre tossed the gown on the bed. "What do you want?"

"Perhaps I should call you Lady Karre." Tomes laughed, pushing off the wall. "That is what they call you here, isn't it?"

"Call me what you wish. I'm used to many names." She shrugged a shoulder. "What do you want, Tomes?"

"I must say you have done quite nicely for yourself. I'm not surprised. Women like you tend to make your way to the top no matter where you go. Though, I will admit, I had hoped you would end up the wife of a mucker, but then this place," Tomes gave a disdainful look around, "is hardly civilized. Even the lords and ladies are primitive, living by fire and sword. How hard it must be for you knowing of the worlds you have seen, knowing of the things you done. I could never live here."

"What do you want, Tomes?" she repeated.

"Want?" He chuckled. "I will give these Starians one thing. They do know how to dress their women." His eyes dipped over her. Karre didn't move. "The men are a little too muscled for my taste, but I saw a few skirts I wouldn't mind plundering. There is nothing sexier than a lush woman forced to bend to my will."

"I'm really not interested in your sex life, so I will ask one last time, what do you want, Tomes?"

His cold gaze grew colder still. "What have you done with the information you have stolen? We've traced every jump in your history. You never go to the same place twice, but we know you have documents. Where are they? Are you working with someone?"

"What reason would I possibly have to tell you?" she asked. Her eyes roamed to the wrist device and her fingers flexed, eager to touch it, to possess it. They would never find where she had gone or how she hid her tracks.

Tomes followed her attention down his arm. "Interestingly enough, when we traveled to where you had been, we noticed something. This device rewrites itself. There is no way of telling where it's gone without the code to reset it. We realized the only way we're going to find our documents is if you take us. Ingenious of you, really. I'm impressed. But then again, I am smarter."

"Modest, too," she mumbled sarcastically.

"I knew there was a reason to keep you alive, a reason far greater than trading for warm water." Tomes drew near, too near for her liking. He looked, but he made no move to touch her.

"You say you're smart, but you keep making me repeat myself," Karre mumbled, before saying very slowly, "What reason would I possibly have to tell you? What is in it for me?"

"Help me and I'll get you off this plane."

"One plane is as good as any other," she said, nonchalantly. "You would have to do better than that."

"Then help me or I'll kill everyone on this plane and leave you to rot here alone or at the mercy of anyone I choose to send here to join you." His slow smile and narrowed gaze made more promises than his words ever could. "Is that better?"

"You've had your look." Karre reached for her gown and stepped back. She tugged it on. The loose material billowed around her without the aid of a corset. "What exactly do you propose? I know I can't trust you."

"Oh, I'm hurt," he said in feigned shock. When she didn't react, he smiled. "It's simple. You don't have a choice in the matter. Come with me, be a good girl and I let you live."

"An offer I can't refuse," she muttered, knowing his words weren't an idle threat.

Tomes reached for his wrist. "Get ready to travel, Lady Sparkles. You have one last job to do. Save this world or I will destroy it."

VIDAR COULD BARELY BREATHE. The guilt and worry ate a constant knot in his stomach and settled a permanent weight over his heart. Karre was gone, vanished like a wood spirit into the night forest. He had looked everywhere, questioned everyone. Beyond a few people saying they saw her walking alone from the courtyard to the castle, there was no sign of her—no tracks, no fairy rings she could have slipped through, nothing. He would have yelled at the knights manning the wall, but he had only ordered them to make sure Karre was well, not to keep her prisoner. For all they knew, she had been participating in some otherworlder ritual.

One conclusion could be drawn. His stubborn wife had talked about infiltrating Magda's encampment and she must have put her plan into motion. But how did she escape the chains? How did she escape an armed fortress full of his knights without being seen?

Already rumors surfaced about Karre's disappearance. The maids claimed she'd been moved to the dungeons. The knights thought the newly married couple played games. Only Synna seemed to have come to the same conclusion as Vidar—Karre went to battle.

He wanted to look for her. His heart ached to do so, but duty demanded he fight. Magda was close. Sorin and his men were ready for battle. The king's orders were clear. His duty to protect his countrymen weighed heavily on him. And in doing his duty perhaps he could somehow find Karre and bring her home. In the end, Vidar spread the rumor throughout Spearhead Fortress that his wife rode out with him to war, to support his efforts and show the Caniba she was not afraid. After what Karre told Synna and the others was spread about, his claim would be believed.

Gods curse her! How could she run off? How could she leave me now? Before such an important battle?

Maybe the king's fears were founded and these otherworld women would bring them nothing but trouble. Maybe he worried for naught. Maybe Karre was safe and had merely run away from him. Maybe she was in Magda's clutches right now only feet away from him underground.

Maybe, maybe, maybe!

"Argh!" Vidar screamed, charging his horse forward as the ground began to shake beneath him. The not-knowing ate at him and he turned his frustration to the only thing he could—the battle before him.

He lifted his sword, hacking his way through the surrounding enemy. More Caniba emerged from the ground, covered in dirt as they clawed their way up like a mound of spreading ants. The hairy beasts all looked the same to him—smelly, pelt-covered monsters with sunken eyes and sharpened teeth.

Their hair hadn't seen a comb, ever, and he highly doubted any of them had heard of bathing.

Three days earlier, Sorceress Magda's army had come up from the ground right through the middle of their encampment. Like a giant serpent of dirt snaking through the ground, the topsoil had sucked into a pit taking a few of their men with it. Caniba warriors rose up, splitting Vidar and Sorin's armies in two. Sorin's men were surrounded, fighting with little reprieve an army twice the dwindling size of theirs.

Vidar ordered his men to hold their ground, as they worked their way deeper into Magda's territory. If they found the sorceress, they could end this. The Caniba felt nothing beyond a driving need to please their queen. Without Magda, her minions would become a scattered mess.

With each thrust of his sword, he heard Karre's name whispering through his head. He slayed his enemy, thrusting his sword into flesh, trying not to watch the Canibas' distorted faces, faces that were impassioned even in death. The smell of sweat, blood and dirt filled each gulping breath. Metal hit upon metal, clanging and clashing over the rough terrain of the battlefield. Starians shouted and moaned, the Caniba growled and grunted and all around them men died.

Karre. Karre. Karre, his mind chanted, tormenting him with the knowledge that he didn't know where she was.

Vidar fought harder, yelling an ancient battle cry to the gods. Then a cry sounded, carried on the wind, "To Lord Sorin! He's going for the sorceress!"

Blinking hard as sweat stung his eyes, Vidar took his focus from the immediate area to look at the large picture. He'd been so intent on the fight he hadn't realized they'd met their goal. They'd rejoined with Sorin's men. Vidar swiped his brow, watching as Sorin made his way toward the makeshift throne of Sorceress Magda.

Eerily pristine in her gown of sparkling white, Magda sat on a carved wood platform, lifted up so that she might watch the carnage she had created with the pride of a goddess. Her evil children swarmed around her, a thick, living wall of protection. Dark, smooth hair fell about her shoulders to her waist and the inky depths of her eyes became even more so by the black lines drawn thick around them.

"To Sorin!" Vidar shouted, seeing how close the lord was. If Sorin could get to her, he could end this. Burning, white heat radiated over his stomach as sharp, metal-tipped nails clawed through his tunic to rake his flesh. He grunted, too consumed by the battle to stop and notice the cut, even as he felt blood trickling down his waist.

"To Sorin!" the men caught up his cry. "To a good death!"

"Help him!" Vidar ordered. A blade cut his arm and then his thigh, as he pushed harder and faster. "Fight to Lord Sorin!"

Sorin had broken rank, leaving a tightly formed unit of knights behind him. Caniba soldiers turned their attentions to him. No Starian had ever made it so close to her in battle.

"To Sorin!" the men shouted.

Caniba warriors surrounded the man, bearing down on him. There was no way Sorin could fight his way through the crowd alone. In a bold move, the lord threw his main line of defense, launching his sword through the air at Magda. The swarm took him down before the blade hit its mark.

Vidar pushed forward, feeling his men at his back. Magda screeched, slumping in her throne. Instantly, her men panicked, turning the tide of the battle as they retreated. The battlefield cleared and the Starians gave chase. Finding Sorin on the ground, wounded with claw and teeth marks, Vidar dropped to his knees to check the man.

"He lives," Vidar said. "Find Lance to tend his wounds and then get him to the marsh encampment." To a nearby group, he ordered, "Search the fallen."

Vidar stood as his orders were carried out. He breathed hard and gripped his sword in frustration. With a violent scream, he threw the weapon after the Caniba warriors. The enemy was too far and the blade embedded into the dirt.

Karre. Karre. Karre.

"I've lost her," he whispered, sure he'd never felt anything as painful as the helplessness the idea caused.

Uncharted Dimension, The Dead Plane

BLOOD TRICKLED down Karre's chin, but she refused to swipe it away. Hot wind would dry it soon enough and she wouldn't give Director Tomes the pleasure of seeing her discomfort. The beginning ache of a bruise stretched over her jaw.

The desolate plains of the uncharted dimension

went on for what Karre imagined would be the whole planet. Here Earth was nothing but sand and rock and wind. Nothing grew on the surface and by extension no animals lived. It's why she called it the dead plane. It's why it was the perfect hideout. She had never seen another person there until now.

"I need assurances that you won't leave me here," she said, keeping her emotionless gaze fixed on his face. A man like the director wouldn't expect her to give in too easily. Tomes had brought her himself, not going to a Divinity base for assistance. She wondered which piece of information she had that made him worried enough to come here alone.

Karre wasn't surprised when he hit her again, this time in the ribs. Growling, he waved his laser pistol in her direction. "I said move it."

Karre tried to take a deep breath and coughed. Holding her injured ribs, she stumbled up the side of the rock incline at the base of a lonely mountain in the sandy sea. Her feet slipped on a bed of sand.

"Move," he growled. "No tricks or I will leave you here."

"Yeah, yeah, I'm moving. Next time you want your prisoner to move faster, try not hitting her in the ribs." On the top of the incline, the ground leveled out and she limped toward a small opening in the rock face.

"Oh, you'd be surprised at what I could do with a female prisoner." He chuckled, the dark sound causing a creepy sensation in her stomach. "Or perhaps you wouldn't be surprised, since you already know. Did you like watching my files? Do you know how much men are willing to give to visit my mansion of pleasure? They won't be pleased that you have the contact list."

Karre kept her back to him so he couldn't see her face. She didn't have any idea what he was talking about. But then, to be fair, she hadn't looked at all her stolen files. She just collected them to be analyzed later when she had enough gemstones saved to set up her own personal research base somewhere.

"Are we close?" he asked, when she refused to answer him.

"It's in the cave." She leaned against a boulder and motioned to the entrance. It was evident by this chatty mood that he didn't plan on letting her leave. If he didn't kill her first, he'd leave her here to die. It wouldn't take long, not in the plane's horrible elements.

Tomes motioned for her to go first. "No tricks."

The stone was warm to the touch, almost hot.

Come nightfall the temperature would drop drastically. Very mindful of her footing, she inched inside, turning sideways in the narrower space. Reaching forward into the darkness, her hand hit a tarp. She pulled it aside.

"Wait," Tomes ordered.

"I'm not going anywhere. You have the portal." She stiffened as the tip of his gun pressed into the small of her back. "There's light just inside."

Karre inched forward, reaching around the corner for the old lantern. Finding it, she reached along the side, grabbing a small knife she kept there for situations just like this. Director Tomes truly underestimated her or truly overestimated himself.

Holding the lantern, she turned the knob several times to light it while keeping the small folded knife in her hand. The sharpened side of the blade bent over toward the handle, keeping it from cutting her palm.

A soft glow illuminated her cave. The dingy brown-and-gray rock had been more home to her over the years than any other place. Now, when she thought of home, she thought of piercing eyes flecked with gold, of swords and knives, of castles and thick forests. She thought of strong hands, toe-curling kisses and a deep voice that made her heart thump wildly in her chest.

The cave fanned out in an oval, carved with jagged walls and natural shelves. A stuffed mat had been rolled and stuck in the corner, just in case she ever needed to stay the night. Freeze-dried foodstuffs were buried in a sealed container, as were medical supplies.

"You're going to kill me, aren't you?" Karre frowned and set the light on the ground. Stark, ghoulish shadows formed on his face, but she read the truth in his eyes. "There is no point in denying it. We both know how this game is played."

"Indeed," he agreed.

"What about the Starians? Will you let them live?"

"There's no reason to hurt the Starians. They have proven to be quite useful for a dumping ground. You, Jayne Hart, Lilith Grian." He chuckled. "It worked better than I could have ever hoped. Marriage as a prison. You have to admire the serendipity."

"You are the reason we...?" She frowned. "What did they do?" When he looked like he would refuse to answer, she added, "What does it matter if you tell me? I'm dead anyway."

"Jayne 'The Sweet' Hart lost a fight and in the process lost me a substantial bet. Lilith Grian was a foolish data analyst, logging her little historical notes. She was easily expendable." Tomes looked over Karre. "The other two we sent saw some of our men coming through a portal. Funny how the Starians sent them back. Even if they do talk about what happened to them, no one on their plane will believe them." He started laughing, his eyes tearing up with mirth. "We once kidnapped a bunch of people from some half-developed plane dressed as these gray, big-eyed, big-headed creatures, probed them anally and then set them down naked in random fields. They told the other inhabitants on their plane they were taken by aliens. They still don't know what all that anal probing was about. I swear, we were so drunk. Now that was a video file you should have stolen. It is unforgettable."

"You've got issues, you know that, right?" Karre didn't find the same amusement in his sick games as he did.

"You still don't get it. When we discovered how to jump to new planes, we discovered the potential to become gods. We can go anywhere, do anything and they can't stop us. Sure, some of the corporation tries to install rules and moral codes, but those of us willing to claim our right as gods are truly free."

"I was wrong. You don't have issues—you're just insane." She backed away from him, toward the jagged stone of the cave wall.

His laughter died and he frowned. "Now it's your turn. What made you think you could fight us?"

"You kidnapped people and took them to the gladiator rings," she stated. "You took the wrong person."

"The fights?" His eyes swept over her in new consideration. "We wouldn't have taken you for the rings. I never sent women to that plane. Someone else, perhaps? A friend? A lover?"

"My father." Her hand gripped so tight she wondered if she would be able to make her fingers work. She felt the tears in her eyes, tears of anger, tears for the past.

"Your father?" His initial shock turned to disbelief. "You've caused me all this trouble because I ordered your father taken to the gladiator plane? How did you know it was me? Those files were destroyed."

He'd ordered it? Karre couldn't move.

"Enough small talk." His gun hand jerked, as if

holding back his barely contained urge to shoot. "Where's the stuff?"

"Why should I tell you? I'm dead anyway."

"Do we really need to do this?" He scowled. Then, almost bored, he said, "If you cooperate you die fast. If you don't you die slow and painful. Either way I get what I want." He sighed heavily. "I always get what I want. I'm a god."

Karre fingered the knife in her closed fist, ready to unfold the blade as soon as he turned his back. Her throat dry, she whispered, "Behind that rock."

Keeping his gun trained on her, he moved to look where she pointed. Karre held her breath. Without realizing it, she had begun to shake. Tomes smiled and she knew he must have seen the glint of light coming from a small hole. He reached in to grab it.

A loud pop sounded and she jerked, knowing he had touched the device. The knife dropped from her fingers. Tomes screamed, his body convulsing as it electrocuted him. The portal device on his wrist sparked and smoked. His finger tightened on the trigger and a pulse of light shot out. Karre jumped to the side, but it grazed her flesh, searing her arm. She fell to the ground with a moan, her whole body sore from his earlier beating.

The gun went off a second and third time and

she closed her eyes tight, curling into a ball. She jerked with each shot, knowing it'd be over soon. The electrical charge would not only kill Tomes but it would fry the portal on his wrist. No one knew where she was or where to look for her. She would be trapped there. Alone. Her husband would never know what happened to her.

Vidar, I'm sorry.

Tomes stopped moving and the cave became as silent as a tomb. After a long moment, she crawled toward the rock Tomes had reached behind. She avoided looking at his still face. He had been an arrogant fool. Karre had security protocols set up all over the cave. Did he really think she would risk losing everything she had worked so hard for?

Pulling out a small box shoved in the back, she held it close and went for the key on the other side of the cave. She leaned against the wall, ignoring the pain radiating over her body, and opened it. A single button waited inside. She hesitated before pressing it.

It was done. Her father was avenged. Every piece of information she'd collected over the years went out through a tiny portal, duplicated and sent to predestined planes. There would be no hiding Divinity's secrets now. It was not how she wanted to disperse the information. She had intended to extract a slow, thought-out revenge. This box was her last-option button. And now that it was pressed, everything she'd worked so hard for was done.

"Vidar," she whispered, knowing the plea was hopeless. She dropped the box as a burning light began to flood the cave. Closing her eyes tight, she tried not to cry. "Come get me. I want to come home."

11

But he could not save her and all the pleasure of brief release was replaced by his sense of failure.

She did not return.

Vidar welcomed the hardness that slowly crept over him. It radiated from his broken heart. Hopefully, given time, stone would replace the organ and he'd be free of the pain that now followed him wherever he went. Questions dogged his every moment—both in wake and restless sleep. Where had she gone? What happened to her? Was she alive? Dead? Why did she leave him? Why wouldn't she send word? What should he do? How could he find the unfindable?

Not knowing was slowly killing him. Not having a plan of action to make it right was killing his soul. Warriors needed to act, to fight. He didn't know how to deal with his helplessness. Nothing in his life had prepared him for it.

The only reprieve he got from his torment were those brief moments in his dreams where Karre would come back to him—smiling, naked, soft and warm. She would wake him with her kiss, the caress of her hand, the brush of her body. The dream was so real, he could feel the press of her pussy against him, wet and inviting. He felt her breasts in his palms. He saw her rising over him, taking him in, crying out for more. As the dreams faded, he heard her voice whispering from far away, "Vidar. Vidar. Come for me. Save me." Then he'd come, spilling his seed in his bed.

But he could not save her and all the pleasure of brief release was replaced by his sense of failure.

"DON'T you think you should report it to the king?" Oskar asked, joining Vidar on the battlements.

Vidar stiffened at the man's words, knowing what his friend spoke of—the missing Lady Karre. He'd spent hours on the fortress wall, looking out over the surrounding countryside, watching the far trails for a hint of Karre walking home to him.

"No," Vidar stated flatly.

"We have searched everywhere for her. It's as if she disappeared off this plane, even though we know it's impossible. The only way she can leave is through a fairy ring—and we don't have fairies—or through one of those alien portals. There are no tracks in the forest, no word of her at Battlewar Castle, no sign of her since she walked away from the courtyard. I've been discreet, but people are beginning to talk. The servants whisper about the lady, saying she's run off and that she's been taken." Oskar said. "You cannot bury the truth forever. Something must be said. It's been weeks since—"

Vidar growled, turning on the knight. He grabbed Oskar's tunic and forced him back against the low wall. "What is the truth? I care not what people say." He let go and stepped back. "We will say nothing."

"As you wish." Oskar straightened, not retaliating. Vidar wished he would. He could have used the fight more than the look of pity in the man's eyes.

"I wish for you to do as I say and saddle the horses." Vidar strode away from him, calling over his shoulder, "If a battle does not come to us, I will go to it."

Perhaps in a good death is where I will find you, my lady. For I have looked everywhere else.

KARRE COULD BARELY MOVE, yet she somehow managed to crawl on top of the uncomfortable pile she had made from all her treasures. She had to use the tarp over the cave entrance to secure it, so now sand blew in to choke her lungs. Hugging her limbs around her treasures, she tried not to breathe too deeply. It had been days since she had eaten—a fact that her stomach wouldn't let her forget—and she had drunk the last of her water the evening before.

Tomes' body lay outside, buried by sand. She found it fitting to leave him where no one would come looking, eternally alone. Once concluding he was in charge of the gladiators, she could connect him to other crimes.

But she couldn't think of any of that now. She had to concentrate. The wrist portal hung loose around her arm. There was no guarantee that she had gotten it to work. Or if it did work that it would even send her to the right dimension and space. She could end up in a boiling river or stuck inside one of Spearhead Fortress' walls. Regardless, she had to try. It was her only chance.

"Vidar, I'm coming home," she whispered, activating the device. Light radiated from the wrist portal and a fire burned into her flesh. Defensively, she tightened her arms around herself and closed her eyes. Every cell in her body felt heavy. She couldn't move. No matter how many times she went through, she would never get used to the sensation of being pulled apart at a molecular level. But this time it was worse. The device was unstable and she felt as if her limbs were being ripped off. "Oh please, let me go home."

VIDAR STRODE across his chambers to grab a sword. Oskar waited for him outside with a small contingency of men. Taking it from atop his trunk, he slid the sheath over his shoulder with practiced ease. He would fight every Caniba he came across until he found his wife or died trying.

As he turned, a strange blue light caught his attention. He frowned, watching the bottom edge of Karre's chamber door. Blue shifted to pale green and he rushed toward it. Throwing open the door, he found the source of the glow at the foot of Karre's bed.

Vidar lifted his hand, shading his eyes from the brightness. On instinct, he gripped the hilt of his sword. Suddenly, a solid mass formed in the light, hovering over the ground before dropping a couple inches to thud onto the floor.

As the light faded, he dropped his arm. "Karre?"

Could it really be her? His heartbeat quickened in relief and worry. Confusion made it hard to move, but he still found the will to step forward.

She didn't answer, didn't move or make a sound. Her face was turned from him and she lay on top of a strange, uneven mass. Smoke curled from a bracelet on her arm and he smelled the unmistakable stench of seared flesh. He hurried to her side, pulling the hot metal from her skin. It had burned its shape into her arm, blistering the flesh.

"Karre?" Vidar pulled her toward him, cradling her in his arms. He brushed the hair from her face. She was thin, her skin tight against her face. His heart beat hard and his fingers shook as he lifted them to her throat. He felt her pulse. "Karre, look at me. Open your eyes."

Lashes fluttered but then settled. Without

opening her eyes, she moaned. He gasped to hear it, relieved that she lived. Nothing else mattered.

She asked weakly, "Did I make it? Am I home?"

"You're home, love, you're home," he murmured, holding her tighter.

You're home, love, you're home.

Karre heard his voice, as it came from far away. Another dream? Or was he real? Vidar would never call her "love", but she was too weak to fight the small grain of hope. If she were dying, then why not let the warmth of his arms and the sound of his loving voice be the last thing she felt? It beat pain and starvation.

Her body ached, her arm burned and the rough trip through the portal made every inch of her insides feel as if they had been ripped apart. She was lifted up and cradled into safety and warmth. Her mind slipped, content to fall into darkness.

Vidar did not leave Karre's side, not when he carried her toward the hall, ordering a servant to find a medic and bring food, not when he laid her on his bed, not when he gently bathed her, not when her eyes opened and they forced broth into her, not when she whimpered throughout the night. Between burns, cuts, bruises and starvation, she had been through a terrible ordeal.

It wasn't until the second night that she managed to keep her eyes open and her thoughts coherent. Seeing her looking up at him as he stroked her cheek, he couldn't help but smile. "You're alive."

"I don't feel very alive." She chuckled. Her hand landed gently on his, holding it to her cheek. "Tell me I'm not dreaming. Tell me you're really here and that I'm really home."

Pleasure erupted inside him when he heard her voice. It filled him with a joy he had never known. It was hard to be demanding and angry about her leaving when she was in his arms, looking at him with those seductively beautiful eyes.

"You're not dreaming. I'm here. You're here. We're together," he assured her. "Where did you go, Karre? I looked for you. I searched everywhere, but we couldn't find any tracks. Why didn't you tell me you were leaving? Was it because I tried to stop you from going?"

"No. It's not your fault. It had nothing to do with our argument or that stupid incident in the court-yard. I'm almost embarrassed thinking of how ridicu-lous we were being. I just wanted so bad to help you, help the people of Staria, help make Spearhead safe."

Vidar leaned his forehead against her temple. "Can you understand that I can't allow you to fight the Caniba? Everything I've ever learned says I have to protect you. If something happens to you, I will have failed in my duty as a warrior. My honor demands I do not fail you. But it's more than that. I couldn't bear it if something happened to you. I'd rather fight to the death a thousand times than let you walk within a hundred yards of Sorceress Magda."

"I understand." She nodded. "But it is not in my nature to do nothing. I won't try to infiltrate her encampment. However, I would like to help."

"My lady, I—"

"I won't do anything without coordinating with you first," she assured him.

"There is time to discuss this later. Right now I would hear where you went. What happened?" He didn't want to let her go so he held on tighter.

"There was no time. I didn't have a choice. I had to go," Karre sighed, dropping her hand from his to rest on the bed. "There was something I had to take care of."

"Because of Magda?"

"No, I had to go to another plane. I needed to finish what I started. I sent files detailing several of Divinity's underhanded deals to my contacts and various media centers on numerous planes. I gave the dimensions proof. Now it is up to them to do something about it." She closed her eyes. Vidar listened as she told him of Divinity's Director Tomes, of how he'd come for her and forced her to go to the dead plane where she'd kept the hidden treasures now in her room. She told him of how she'd avenged her father by causing the death of the man responsible. "The portable jump prototype was fried when Tomes' sins came back to him. I managed to fix it for one last jump by scavenging parts from the other devices I've collected."

"The thing on your wrist?" He lifted her arm to kiss near the healing burn.

"Yes. I wasn't sure it would work." She caressed his face. "I cannot believe it did work. I really thought I would never see you again. The odds of my ending up here," she coughed, her eyes watering. "I should have gone to another dimension. I should have ended up trapped in a stone wall. I wasn't even sure I had the directions inputted right."

"I told you the gods have their reasons. They brought you to me a second time. They know that you belong with me." Vidar kissed her forehead. "And I belong with you. None of those other things could have happened because we are fate."

"Fate?" She moaned softly. "I like the sound of that."

"So do I." Vidar brought his lips to hers.

Karre drew strength from his presence. She was still sore from her ordeal, but it didn't matter. The wounds would heal. By some miracle, she had made it home to him and that's all that mattered. She dug her fingers into his hair, gripping tight, as if he might slip away into a dream and she would wake up alone.

"I thought I'd never see you again." She pushed at him, drawing strength from his nearness. Rolling him on his back, she tugged at his tunic, needing to feel his flesh.

"As did I." Vidar leaned up and lifted his arms, letting her undress him. "I have never felt such fear."

Passion and need filled her, fueled by the fear she had carried while stuck on the dead plane. She kissed him, devouring his mouth with hers. Every moment they were together had filtered through her thoughts while she was away and they now poured into their kiss. She loved everything about him—his smell, his taste, the way his brow furrowed when he was arguing with her, the way his eyes smiled when he looked at her from across a room.

Urgency filled them. They tore at each other's clothing, ripping the material in their haste. Karre gasped as her breasts rubbed against his firm chest. His masculine scent surrounded her and she breathed deeply. She straddled his thighs, leaning into his rising cock. It pressed into her stomach.

Karre eagerly explored his body, trying to touch every ounce of flesh. Anticipation washed over her, centering on her pussy and breasts. She wanted to feel him and needed him to feel her. He pushed her up to give himself better access to her chest.

Vidar groaned, rolling her over. Strong fingers rubbed her breasts in firm strokes, budding her nipples into his palms. Their legs tangled in the covers. She worked her feet along his calves in an effort to free their limbs. Once free, Karre hooked her legs around his waist. She reached between them, taking his cock to stroke the turgid length. Her hand bumped into her sex, giving herself pleasure as she touched him. She arched her hips upward, letting her clit rub against her hand. A jolt of pleasure racked through her with each pass.

He licked the corner of her mouth, trailing wet kisses over her jaw from her chin to her earlobe. He thrust a finger into her sex, wiggling it until she panted in desperation for more. She spread her legs wider, inviting more.

He bit her lobe. "I want to be inside you. I burn for you."

"Then take me." She took her hand from him, moaning in encouragement. "Take all of me. I never want to be without you again, Vidar. I love you."

He looked as if he would speak, but he'd already slid his cock along her slick folds. She thrust up, urging him inside her. His hips propelled forward, fitting himself to the hilt. Vidar rocked on top of her, taking her slow and easy, as if he was afraid of breaking her. He braced his arms on either side of her, keeping his perfect rhythm as he thrust in and out, in and out.

Karre held on tight, unable to take her eyes off him. Firelight danced on his tight flesh but was nothing compared to the inner fire in his eyes. His name left her lips with a pleasured groan. Seconds later, she came, trembling in violent release. He stiffened, jerking as he too met his end.

When the climatic tremors receded, he fell to her side and gathered her against him. He kissed her temple, keeping her close. "I don't know when or how, but I love you, too, my lady. When you were gone I felt as if my whole world no longer mattered. I will give anything to make you happy, just don't leave me again. All I have is yours. I love you, Karre, forever."

No words could describe the feelings that erupted inside her at his admission. Turning to face him, she grinned, "Now I know I didn't make it through the portal. This is too perfect to be real."

KARRE LAUGHED as she pulled a piece of torn parchment out of her shoe. For the first time in weeks, she felt great. The bruises and cuts had healed. Even the burn on her arm no longer ached, though it had formed into a scar around her wrist. Oddly enough, the mark only seemed to draw the esteem and compliments of the Starian knights. Rolling the parchment in her fingers, she said, "I know where the Divinity portal is hidden."

Behind her place on the floor, Vidar stopped moving. An easiness had developed between them, an understanding that didn't always need words. But it was more than that. There was trust. She glanced over her shoulder, seeing him near the bed. Slowly, he pulled his tunic over his head. "Oh?"

Karre closed her eyes and pretended to concentrate. "It's true. I saw it. It is to the north." She peeked at him, trying not to laugh at his confused expression. "Yes, north. Battlewar Castle. Dungeon." She again peeked at him. Confusion turned to worry. "No, hold on a moment, it's the old dungeons." Worry faded into concern. "And," Karre paused, lifting the piece of paper to read, "Last door, down stairs..." She started laughing, unable to continue as realization replaced his small frown. Shaking the small note, she said, "Lilith left me directions to Divinity's headquarters so I could escape you."

Vidar strode to her and reached to help her to her feet. "Escape, my lady? Never."

"Never," she agreed, standing next to him. She wrapped her arms around his neck. Meeting his lips, she kissed him briefly. "We should go. The device is ready."

"Are you sure this is what you want to do? I still do not like taking you over the border." He placed his hands along her hips, sliding them back to rest on the small of her back. "I'd rather keep you here."

"We've discussed this," Karre said, "at length."

Vidar nodded. She knew he didn't like it, but at least he wasn't forbidding her to go with him. "Gather what you need. I will ready the horses."

12

Because right now, in this moment, Karre no longer had a role to play.

The stagnant air as they traveled through the marshes made it hard to breathe. Moss-covered trees surrounded them, creating a curtain along the narrow trail of dry land. Karre let the horse make its own way as it walked behind Vidar's mount and before Oskar's. Both men had assured her that the Caniba would not rise up from the water. Even with their reassurances, she found herself constantly tense and straining to see peeks of landscape beyond the mossy veil.

"Are we close?" Karre asked, wishing she'd

shared a horse with Vidar. She could use the comfort of his body. He'd refused, saying he'd be better able to protect her if his limbs were free to fight.

"One minute closer from when you asked a minute ago," Vidar said, looking back. Concern shone through his handsome eyes and she knew with one word she could make him forget this course of action.

A nervous tension rolled through her. Never had the stakes been so high. Everything she loved depended on her abilities and the idea of failing Vidar terrified her more than being trapped on a dead plane, more than capture by Divinity, more than death itself. Because right now, in this moment, Karre no longer had a role to play. This wasn't an act. She wasn't in character. This was her life. Everything she could ever want. If she failed...

It will not fail, she told herself, refusing to think of it again.

THE HORSES SPLASHED through the shallow marsh waters, past small patches of earth sticking up in random patterns. Vidar's horse led hers to higher ground, to the town of rectangular tents bathed in moonlight and firelight. The smell of burning wood from the bonfires dominated the evening. Tiny, orange sparks from the flames danced in the evening sky before dying out.

Karre reached behind her, patting the satchel that hung against her horse. It bounced with each movement, but she'd padded the contents inside to keep them safe. As the ground leveled and they entered the camp, Vidar reined his mount next to hers.

The tents, varying in sizes, spread out over the high clearing on an orderly grid to create pathways. The larger tents were in the middle with progressively smaller ones fanning round them. Banners hung from the tent flaps, pinned to the opened entryways. Their brilliant colors stuck out against the light caramel of the canvas.

"The Caniba prisoner is here?" she asked.

"He is," Vidar acknowledged.

"Then let's get started. I don't want to wait." Karre let go of the satchel.

Vidar dismounted and moved to help her down. "This way, my lady."

Vidar did not like his wife's presence in the encampment, but he was proud of her for coming.

He knew how important it was for her to belong in her new world—to help, to prove herself worthy. She was worthy—he tried to tell her as much but she needed to feel it.

Oskar stayed behind with the horses as Vidar grabbed the satchel and walked her toward a nearby tent. Two men guarded the front flap, with more around the sides.

"Careful, Sir Vidar, the madness is deepening in him," one of the guards said. "He cries for his queen."

Vidar nodded. Karre appeared brave, but he knew the truth. He saw her hands tremble ever so slightly, saw the hesitance in her eyes as he opened the front flap to the holding tent. Dirt floors stretched along the entire length, worn smooth by the constant brush of feet over the earth. In the center, their Caniba prisoner was tied to a thick wooden chair, which had been weighted by lead shoes bolted to each leg. The light was dim, kept purposefully so. Bright lights seemed to aggravate their prisoner. Not that the harsh, rapid breath resounding over the space could be considered relaxed. It sounded more like a rabid dog caught in a trap. Perhaps that was exactly what their prisoner was.

As his eyes adjusted to the dim light, he saw Karre make a move to step past him. He held out his arm, stopping her. "Tell me what needs to be done and I will do it."

"Hand me my bag," she said. He did and she knelt on the floor to rummage through it. She kept glancing toward the center chair.

The Caniba stared back at her with ravenous eyes. His jaw moved in slow bites, working open and closed. A deep scar ran along the man's cheek, down across his chin and back up the other side. His hair bunched around his head in tight knots and frayed strands. He didn't smell as bad as the others because one of the Starian knights had doused him with soapy water.

Vidar stepped in front of his wife, blocking her from view as she busied herself putting together her device. She'd been working on it since she'd gotten back, spending endless hours adjusting and readjusting. Vidar had built catapults, forged weapons and strategized battles, but he'd never seen anything as confusing as the inner workings of her contraptions.

"Ready." Karre stood and handed him an alien device. It looked like a metal helmet with strange carvings and protrusions all over it. "Put it on his head. I'll do the rest."

As Karre tried to put a matching device on her own head, he ordered, "No. I thought we agreed that

I would take on the prisoner's memories. I do not wish for you to see such things."

"I never said that specifically," Karre denied. "Put it on him. I know how to navigate to find the memories we need. I can do it faster."

"But you said they happen as visions. I know this land. I know where the visions will lead," Vidar argued.

The Caniba growled at Karre, "I will feed you to my queen."

"Charming." She dismissed the prisoner, still not getting too close. To Vidar, she said, "I'll describe it in full detail. Put it on him."

Instead of instantly obeying, he leaned into her and kissed the corner of her mouth. "If it becomes too much..."

"I know. I'll stop. I promise." Karre slipped the helmet on her head, adjusting it.

Karre couldn't stop, no matter how depraved she felt on the inside. She felt the Caniba's hunger. It built up inside of him like a disease, festering, oozing, consuming the soul like a demonic poison. When he was away from his queen, a physical pain came over him.

"He doesn't have a name. None of them have

names. Not anymore, not that they can remember, not that they care to. Magda drugs them," Karre said, keeping her eyes closed and her thoughts focused on traveling through the enemy's brain. She saw the Caniba queen in a large stone cavern. Torchlight surrounded her throne, shining off her white gown like a million tiny stars. Oddly clean amongst the dirty obsession of her followers, Magda carried herself like royalty.

"Karre?" Vidar's voice penetrated the heavy fog.

"She puts the drug into her cup and offers it to her warriors as a reward. One taste and they are addicted. It keeps them loyal," Karre continued. She smacked her lips, as her mouth filled with a salty-metal memory of the sacred Caniba wine coated her tongue. "She serves it in blood." A rush of pleasure filled Karre, streaming over her entire body. "It feels wonderfully euphoric. It's in my blood. It feels like I'm flying and spinning and dancing. The pull is too strong. There is no cure for it. We must obey my queen."

Karre felt the press of the other followers against her arms. She would give her life for the bloodthirsty sorceress, commit any deed.

"Try to find where she's hidden," Vidar instructed.

The prisoner growled from his place on the chair and tried to fight Karre's mental probing. She pulled her thoughts from the ceremony, not having realized just how far she'd slipped into the sorceress' spell.

"I'm coming from the mouth of a cave. She's ordered me to the borderlands. Already the fear and hunger grow in my stomach. I must please her so she will reward me." Karre clenched her fists tight. Her head began to throb. She'd modified the memory implanter to let her access his mind. The device wasn't supposed to work like this—keeping people connected for so long. It was supposed to upload memories and then quickly implant them.

"I hear water. It's the queen's bathing pool. We're not allowed to use it, but we can watch." A sharp pain shot through her head and she cried out.

"End it," Vidar demanded.

"I almost have it," Karre gasped. "It's a waterfall. Big. There's a crooked tree several miles away."

Karre screamed and clawed at her head, fumbling for the button to turn the device off. Vidar's hands were on the helmet, lifting it off as soon as it deactivated. Chanting filled her, echoing from the prisoner's mind. Her vision swam, causing her world to teeter out of control.

"Karre? Karre?" Vidar sounded so worried. His arms were around her—safe, secure, forever.

The pain was too much. It radiated all over her. She answered the only thing she could. "I will feed you to my queen."

Vidar gathered Karre into his arms and carried her from the tent. A trail of blood streaked down her cheek from her nose. She didn't move, but he'd heard her last words clearly.

I will feed you to my queen.

The words chilled him. He'd seen the blank look in her eyes, heard the desperate pain in her voice. Why had he let her convince him to do this? What if the Caniba's thoughts didn't leave her? What if she went crazy? He should have asked more questions about the device. She'd made it seem so harmless, as if she'd done it a thousand times.

"Grab the lady's bag," Vidar ordered the guard. "Send Lance to my tent."

As Vidar carried his wife toward his usual tent, he saw a couple of men coming out of it. He nodded, knowing they hadn't been given much warning about their leader's arrival. Rushing her inside, he laid her down on the narrow bed.

The redheaded Lance appeared holding a device

much like the ones Karre had. "Step back, Sir Vidar. I will scan her."

Vidar hesitated, but finally stepped back to let the medic work. "What is that thing?"

"Lady Lilith retrieved this handheld scanner for us from a medical plane and gave it to me at the Fire Ceremony. It was used on Lord Sorin's battle injuries and even his scars were removed. Lady Lilith trained me how to use it. If my report to the king is favorable, we'll be able to trade for more. Already it has saved lives, mended bones, broken fevers." Lance lifted the unit over his unmoving wife. "What happened?"

"She was injured by alien technology." Vidar's gut tightened. "Let us hope she can be saved by it."

MY QUEEN!

Karre gasped, pressing her temple. The echoing demands of the Caniba prisoner's memories screamed in her head, filling her with a desperate ache, and she'd only glimpsed into the man's brain. She couldn't imagine what it would be like to actually be drugged into submitting to Sorceress Magda's will.

"Karre?" Vidar whispered, concerned.

She blinked, trying to push the feelings aside. Her eyes focused on his handsome face. "I'm all right." Karre reached for him, holding onto his shoulders. "Come here. I need to feel something warm." After the coldness of the Caniba, it was true. "I need you."

She barely registered their surroundings, not caring that the voices of knights sounded outside their tent. Vidar captured and held her attention. Cream instantly pooled along her folds, wetting her sex.

Karre took a deep breath, realizing her corset had been loosened while she was passed out. She moved on the bed, liking the way the stiff material brushed her nipples, caressing them with each hurried breath.

"You had me worried," he said, his hand on her hip inching up her skirt. His eyes drifted over her length to briefly pause on her chest before again meeting her gaze. "Promise me you are done and that you will leave the fighting to me from now on."

"I promise no such thing," she whispered. Karre smiled at him, moving gently along his body as he settled against her. She reached for her skirt, pulling it up faster so that she could freely move her legs. Desire and passion built, coursing through her until she thought she might explode with the intensity of it. Then she set to work on his breeches, tugging the laces at his waist. Her hand slid next to his arousal. "Mm, you're so warm. I ache for you. Come here."

"Are you sure you're well?" Vidar glanced at the tent flap, as if he expected someone to walk in.

"No. I know I am not." Karre squirmed, parting her legs. Her body tingled, each nerve alive. "I need you inside me, warrior. Now." She licked her lips, keeping them parted.

"Whatever my lady wishes." His body shifted and he lifted over her, settling between her thighs. She shoved his breeches down his hips, freeing him enough to allow their bodies access. He slid his hand down her side. "I am powerless against you."

The thick tip of his cock probed her pussy, gliding along her slit before finding aim. He thrust into her. Her heartbeat quickened, pounding in her chest. She inhaled deeply.

He took her slow and sweet, letting her feel every agonizing moment. When she was with him, everything else faded away. She breathed in his scent, felt the press of his body, the warmth of his nearness, the taste of his kiss.

Karre angled her hips, silently urging him to go faster. He gave her what she wanted, driving forward, sliding, pounding, harder and faster. She gasped, desperate to find her release.

She bit her lip, moaning loudly as she reached her climax. The muscles of her pussy quivered, gripping his cock as he buried himself deep. Vidar shuddered, letting loose a loud groan as he came. Karre giggled, not caring who heard them.

"I love you, my lady," Vidar whispered, lying next to her on the small bed.

Karre smiled and closed her eyes. A sudden shot of pain went through her and she gasped, grabbing her head. Flashes came to her, dark and twisted. Vidar's voice was far away, but she heard his panic. She felt the brush of stone against her hand, damp and cold. Blinking hard, she said, "I know where the queen lives."

VIDAR DIDN'T LIKE TAKING his wife with him past the borderlands into Caniba land, but they needed her implanted visions to find their way through the twisted maze of stone and forest. And navigate she did, leading them through the countryside as if she were native to the land. He worried about her, saw the faded light in her eyes right before she told them where to go.

"This is it," Karre whispered, pointing toward the sound of running water. She lay on the ground next to him and the small contingency of knights with them. Thick shrubs hid them from the Caniba. Aside from the plant life, the forest seemed dead, devoid of even the smallest of animals. The only sound beyond the wind was the low hum of insects. "She lives behind the waterfall. I don't know what's past there, but she'll be there."

Vidar nodded. "You have done well, my lady. Now it is time for you to go."

"What?" Her rounded eyes looked into his. "I'm not going anywhere."

"I won't fight about this now. You've done well and brought great honor to our name. You showed us the way. Now I need you back in the safety of the encampment." Vidar knew before she even opened her mouth that she would argue with him. He nodded to Oskar. The man, having his orders, took Lance's handheld medic unit and pressed it against Karre's arm. Her mouth opened but only a soft wheeze sounded as she passed out.

"My lady will not be happy when she wakes up," Oskar said.

"But she'll be safe," Vidar answered. "I'm entrusting you to take her to the marsh encampment."

Oskar nodded, gathering Karre into his arms. Vidar waited several minutes, giving them time to get away before turning his attention back to the waterfall. He'd miss Oskar's sword and knew the man gave up much in turning away from the battle to protect a lady. But Oskar, like all Starians, knew the importance of such a task. To the three remaining knights he said, "At the ready, men. In there lies a great victory to this war."

Two DEAD AND one injured out of four. Vidar looked down at his bloody arm and frowned as he flexed his tingling hand. Next to him, Luca remained unharmed. The two fallen were laid along the narrow cave next to their killers.

Green light shone over the cave, emanating from worms in a trench along either side of the natural pathway. A sickeningly strange combination of flowers and unwashed bodies filled the cave air, as if someone used heavy perfume to cover the need for a bath. Steadying his breath, he motioned Luca to continue.

Without hesitation, the man surged forward, sword held high. The passageway opened up into a large cavern. Luca lifted his hand. Vidar crept forward and stopped. Inside the sparse room, Magda crouched alone in the center of a circle. Her back was to them, but Vidar recognized the pristine white of her gown—strange in such a dirty home. He could see her bare feet firmly planted.

Luca moved forward, stealthily placing his feet on the ground. Vidar joined him, circling the sorceress in the opposite direction. She stiffened. The knights stopped. Luca pulled a knife from his waist and threw it at the woman. Magda screeched, surging to her feet. As she stood, the sorceress revealed the front of her gown. The white was stained crimson, as were the woman's face and hands. She caught the knife's hilt with lightning speed, spinning it around in her hand before launching it back at Luca. The knife embedded in his shoulder and he stumbled back.

Magda screeched again, the sound high and long, baring four perfect fangs amidst her teeth. When she looked at him, her eyes shifted color, filling with eerie golden threads. Her hands spread out to her sides, as if daring him to try. Vidar grabbed his knife and threw. Instead of waiting for it to hit its target, he charged the queen while her attention was focused on catching the blade. As the knife landed against her palm, she turned. Vidar thrust his sword. His blade missed, slicing through her dark hair. He saw Luca stand, the man's arm limp.

There was an odd grace to the way Magda fought, as if she had no fear of death or pain. It was very unlike the brute style of the Caniba. She leapt and spun, landing with ease on her bare feet only to twirl in the opposite direction. Vidar tried to chase after her, but she was too fast, dodging his best swings. No human he'd ever seen could move like that.

Luca growled, jerking the knife from his shoulder to throw at the woman as she sped past. It hit her arm, but she kept going. She jumped, screeching as she sprang off the cave wall before landing behind Luca. Grabbing Luca's head, she bit into his neck with a vicious rip. Vidar ran. Luca dropped to the ground, unmoving.

Magda flew at him, bloody mouth wide open. With inhuman strength, she flung him across the room. When she came at him again, he lifted his sword and embedded it in her stomach. Even stabbed, she didn't stop. Vidar grabbed her throat, holding her fangs back seconds before they sank into his flesh. They rolled over the stone floor. As his back hit, the sword blade slid up her stomach. Her strength waned. Vidar grabbed the hilt and jerked. Her eyes widened as it hit her heart. She stopped moving. Then, as if she'd never been there, her body turned to ash, which rained down on top of him. The sorceress was dead.

Coughing, he grabbed his arm and struggled to his feet. He reached for his neck, feeling the sticky blood where her teeth had scraped. He could barely lift his sword as he stumbled toward the entrance. If he didn't get out of there soon, he'd be dead too.

I'LL KILL HIM!

Karre pushed up from the fur rug on the ground, ready to storm out of the encampment tent and back over the borderlands. She knew the way now. It was imprinted in her head. At least the insistent screaming of the Caniba's pain had left her mind. As she made her way to the door, she skidded to a stop. Vidar was there, lying on the bed. He looked bloodied and bruised.

"Vidar!" She hurried to him, all anger replaced by the sight of him. He didn't move, as his chest rose in shallow breaths. How long had she been out? What happened? She remembered being shot with the handheld medical unit. Had they been attacked? She briefly felt his forehead, noting the intense heat. Frowning, she hurried for the tent flap. Seeing Oskar next to several riders, she beckoned the man over.

Oskar ordered the riders to go and they took off in different directions.

"What's happened?" Karre demanded. "Another attack?"

Oskar grinned. It was a look she'd never seen on the man. "I sent word to the castles. Magda is dead. Vidar has done it. You have done it, my lady." Those who heard the knight began to cheer in excitement. The wave washed over the entire encampment. "Her spell is broken. The prisoner in the tent has calmed. He had no idea where he is or what happened to him. It is the same for those in Magda's camp. They don't know who they are. Vidar crawled out of the queen's cave and they simply laid down their arms. Magda's spell is broken. I've even sent word to have Fredrick released. Synna will be very happy to have him home."

Karre stood in shock before turning to look at the

tent. "Where is Lance? Vidar needs help. He needs—"

"Lance is on his way. Vidar will live. Go, be with him. I'll send the medic as soon as he arrives." Oskar turned, shouting in victory to again make a wave of sound over the encampment as others joined him.

Karre went back to the tent and to Vidar's side. She brushed the hair back from his forehead. "I can't believe you drugged me to face her alone."

"I wasn't alone," he mumbled, not opening his eyes. "I had three good men with me who gave their lives for the fight."

She let loose a long breath to hear his voice, even if it was hoarse. Frowning, she saw punctures at his neck and gently turned his head to the side. "Who bit you?"

"Magda tried." This time he did open his eyes, weakly reaching to grab her hand and pull it from his jaw. "She was very strong. She kept fighting even after I ran her through. I have never seen anything like it. Then she just stopped."

"Did she stop after you stabbed her in the heart?" Karre rested her palm against his chest, feeling his heart beat.

Vidar nodded. "I saw the death in her eyes and then she turned to dust."

"Vampire," Karre said. "It makes complete sense. She must have come here through a fairy ring just like others. She used her blood to enslave the Caniba to her will. That is why they've gone crazy and can't remember who they are now that her hold over them is broken. Her power was in her blood. When you killed her, you ended that power."

"Vampire?"

Karre sighed thoughtfully. "I've only met a few on Plane 395, but they were in the Adult Pleasure Center VWH—that's vampires, werewolves, humans. They were relatively harmless, but I've heard stories of other, darker creatures. They're undead, supernatural beings, nearly impossible to kill and they survive by drinking the blood of the living. She could have been here for centuries, ruling the Caniba, asserting her hold over them, making them bring her live food offerings. It makes sense that she's in the earth, too. That kind prefers to live in the ground."

"They let our men pass to pick up our dead without a fight. They seemed more confused than anything." Vidar tried to sit up, but she pressed on his chest to keep him down.

"Sir Vidar," Lance interrupted, coming into the tent. Seeing Karre, he added, "My lady."

Karre stepped away, hovering as Lance set to work mending Vidar's wounds. When the man had finished and left, she stopped him from getting up by crawling on top of him and pinning him to the bed. "I'm not happy with your decision to drug me and cart me back here."

"I did what I had to. I needed to know you were safe." He ran his hands along her hips. Though still visible, his wounds no longer looked as bad as they had been.

"Oh, I'll forgive you eventually, but you're going to have to work for it." She laughed as he quickly flung her onto her back.

"As you wish, my love," he said before he kissed her. "As you wish."

EPILOGUE

Because right now, in this moment...

Karre smiled in pride as she watched her husband being granted a lordship by the Starian king. He'd fought well and bravely and deserved the honor and the permanent bequeathment of Spearhead.

Battlewar Castle overflowed with those who'd come to celebrate Magda's demise. The war was over, a thing not all of the Starians were prepared to accept. But with Magda's hold over the Caniba gone, the enemy had lost their will to fight. It was more than could have been hoped for. They all knew how important and formidable the sorceress was, but no one had known what she was or that she'd come from another plane. With her death came peace and a whole race of warriors with no idea what to make of their lives without a battle.

"I've been authorized by the king to begin renegotiating bridal trade," Lilith said, glancing across the low table at Karre. Jayne and an obviously pregnant Paige had joined them at the table. "With Director Tomes missing and some sort of disruption at the company, I think we can pretty much get anything we want."

Karre hid her smile.

"Just make sure the women know what they're getting themselves into," Jayne said, subtly wiggling her fingers in her husband, Lord Ronen's direction. Five young boys stood next to him. They were Jayne and Ronen's adopted children.

"Impossibly stubborn men who no longer have a war, so they turn their attentions to their wives." Paige laughed, gently rubbing her stomach. "Not that I complain at Aidan's attentions."

"I might even open up trade with other dimensions, if anyone here has any requests or ideas," Lilith added.

"I might have a few," Karre answered, trying not to show her amusement. "More medic units, food synthesizers, massage booths, oh, and there is this great shoemaker on Plane 45 who makes wonderful boots. They fit the foot like a second skin. I always meant to do more shopping when I was there."

"I'll put it on my list," Lilith drawled.

"Warriors without a war," Jayne mused, standing. "Whatever will we do with them?"

"I'm going to go lie down," Paige said, waving over Aidan to join her.

Karre turned her full attention forward, smiling at Vidar as he made his way toward her. The main hall faded away as she looked at him. Her breathing deepened and her heart quickened, just like the first time she'd seen him in this very castle. His eyes narrowed and firelight reflected off the yellow flecks that ringed his irises. Everything about him captured her senses.

"Well done, my sir." She bit her lip and pressed her legs tightly together, trying to tame the sexual desire she felt for him. It was no use. She found her gaze going to the bulge between his thighs—strong, muscular thighs surrounded a thickening cock.

"Actually, that would be my lord," he corrected. She took his hand and followed him as he led her through the hall. Once there, he swept her into his arms.

"You know, I've never slept with a lord before." Karre kissed his neck.

"We'll have to rectify that, my lady. After tonight, you will never sleep without a lord again." And with that he whisked her down the hall.

The End

ARIELLA'S KEEPER

THE SERIES CONTINUES...

Divinity Healers
by Michelle M. Pillow

Alternate Reality Romance

When his father threatens to take away his research facility's funding if he doesn't come home, Dr. Sebastjan Walter has no choice but to do so. This isn't just a family reunion. It seems his father has arranged a marriage—Sebastjan's. Seeing his chance to make one last final deal to get his father out of his life, he agrees to marry the off-plane woman. After seeing her, he can't help but think he's made the better bargain.

Ariella has been held prisoner by the Medical

Supreme since he cured her of a childhood illness. Forced to stay in his home as his ward, she has no choice but to do whatever he wants. When he demands she marry his son, Ariella finds this is one order she might not mind obeying.

ABOUT MICHELLE M. PILLOW

New York Times & *USA TODAY*
Bestselling Author

Michelle loves to travel and try new things, whether it's a paranormal investigation of an old Vaudeville Theatre or climbing Mayan temples in Belize. She believes life is an adventure fueled by copious amounts of coffee.

Newly relocated to the American South, Michelle is involved in various film and documentary projects with her talented director husband. She is mom to a fantastic artist. And she's managed by a dog and cat who make sure she's meeting her deadlines.

For the most part she can be found wearing pajama pants and working in her office. There may or may not be dancing. It's all part of the creative process.

✕

Come say hello! Michelle loves talking with readers on social media!

www.MichellePillow.com

facebook.com/AuthorMichellePillow

x.com/michellepillow

instagram.com/michellempillow

bookbub.com/authors/michelle-m-pillow

goodreads.com/Michelle_Pillow

amazon.com/author/michellepillow

youtube.com/michellepillow

pinterest.com/michellepillow

COMPLIMENTARY EXCERPTS

TRY BEFORE YOU BUY!

LILITH ENRAPTURED

BY MICHELLE M. PILLOW

Divinity Warriors Book One

Alternate Reality Romance

Sorin of Firewall lives in a land forever at war. In fact, the Starian men are so busy fighting, their marriage ceremony has been reduced to a "will of the gods" event where they simply pick a woman out of a lineup and claim her as a wife. With women becoming scarce, it's necessary to trade the offworld Divinity Corporation for brides. Duty-bound to attend the ceremony, he has no intention of picking a bride, let alone one from another dimension. That is, until he sees Lilith, the bewitching woman sent by the gods to reward—or punish?—him.

For a complete, up-to-date booklist, visit www.
MichellePillow.com

FIGHTING LADY JAYNE

THE SERIES CONTINUES

Divinity Warriors Book Two
by Michelle M. Pillow

Alternate Reality Romance

Jayne Hart has earned her independence by becoming Divinity Corporation's inter-dimensional boxing champion. Life is great, until a dirty fighter knocks her unconscious. Now, abandoned by the corporation in a parallel world, Jayne will use every weapon she has to be free once more. Even if it means running from her sexy new "husband" and spending the rest of her life in a primitive forest.

Ronen of Firewall longs for a woman to warm his bed and his home, but he had no intention of choosing a bride. In an unprecedented move, one chooses him. Never in the history of the marriage ceremony has a woman dared to lay claim. How can he resist the alluring Lady Jayne? She's confident and sure in her decision to be with him—until their wedding night when she's nowhere to be found. But, Ronen is not one to shy from a battle. He will find Jayne and, when he does, he has one particular "weapon" in mind for taming his seductive, wayward wife.

Extended Prologue Excerpt

Getting her teeth knocked around in her head hurt like hell, but being able to spit blood into the face of her opponent more than made up for the discomfort. Jayne "The Sweet" Hart laughed as Big Bobby Bishop sputtered in anger. She knew he expected her to cry at the landed blow. Truth was, part of Jayne did want to cry. She wasn't a glutton for a beating, and that last hit had left blood running out of her mouth at a steady flow. They'd been going at it for nearly a half hour, bare-knuckle boxing—no protective gear beyond any sanctioned bioengineering, no referees, not like some of the other dimensions had. No, here on dimensional plane 241 almost anything was legal. That's why the gladiator ring paid such big money and drew the notice of rich, inter-dimensional travelers who could afford a private plane jump through Divinity Corporation. It's also why Jayne agreed to travel from her own world to this alternate reality where laws were more of a suggestion and killing someone in a fight was considered a good thing.

In many ways, each alternate reality was like drifting through time on her own home plane, had a singular event on the timeline been changed. Each dimension seemed to be a different outcome to a similar historical start. Some were so technologically advanced everything was done for them, and they'd found a worldwide peace and understanding. Jayne generally stayed away from those levels of existence. There wasn't much employment for fighters in such realities.

Other planes hadn't even developed a means of fast communication beyond throwing a bird into the air with a tiny letter tied to its leg. Still others had just installed their first aqueducts or invented their first vehicles to run without horses or oxen. Or, like 241, they had every technological comfort and yet

somehow managed to maintain their barbarian sensi-
bilities.

Any way you looked at it, Earth was Earth, just
different versions of itself—same languages, matching
natural events, some people looked the same but
weren't. Humans, for the most part, still resembled
humans. And those with power were still greedy
bastards trying to tell her how to do her job.

Big Bobby watched her expectantly, his mouth
opened as if to scream in victory at any second. Jayne
knew he expected her to fall with that punch. She
watched as the excitement slowly died from his eyes,
replaced by shock, then confusion, until finally a
boiling rage. His eyes scanned the crowd before
moving toward the large balcony to where his daddy
sat watching. Big Bobby's father and known gangster
boss had undoubtedly assured his halfwit-of-a-lug-
nut son that he was a sure winner. It wouldn't have
been so bad if Big Bobby had been an admirable
opponent, but after a half hour, she could still see out
of one of her eyes, and he only managed to knock her
off her feet twice.

And Bossman Bishop wanted her to take a dive
to this chump?

Jayne snorted. Not bloody likely. She'd never
work as a boxer again—not that she had to. In her

home dimension, she had plenty of money to bide her twelve lifetimes.

Divinity Corp paid her big for this fight. They were her ticket home and had the only known source of inter-dimensional travel technology on this plane. Natural slips were extremely rare and the timing of them completely predictable by the company, even if they didn't know where the slip would go. If they didn't take her home, she'd be stuck until the end of time. Besides, there was no way she was taking a dive just because the local gangsters had promised to...

What had Bossman said again? Oh, yeah. They were going to gang rape her grandma while she watched. It had hardly been a threat. Jayne was an orphan. Still, a part of her was up in arms for the hypothetical grandmother they'd threatened.

There was no way Bossman could know about her lack of family. The publicity put out by Divinity Corp's entertainment division fostered the wholesome image of their Sweetheart Jayne. Of course, it was all a lie. They hired a family to take pictures with her at a rented country home—the devoted mother, the fake twin sister with a poor health condition, the baby brother and suit 'n' cravat dad.

The loud, almost fanatical cheering of the crowd grew. They surrounded on all sides, lining the rows upon rows of rotating theater seats. Every few minutes, the seats would shift, changing the angle from which a person watched. Lights flashed all around her. Floating cameras zipped by her head, but she ignored them. Most of the bets were on her and she never lost a fight. Never. And she would be damned if she gave this guy the reputation of being the one person who could take her down. He didn't deserve the title or her respect. Rage grew within her that he even dared to presume he was worthy of taking her down.

Do it for your family, Jayne, she thought sardonically.

Jayne decided to teach him and Bossman a lesson. She drew her body around, preparing to kick him upside the head in a move she knew he wouldn't see coming. Big Bobby swung again. She dodged the blow, and this time his hand merely grazed her cheek, stinging the cut she had there. She didn't hesitate. Whipping her leg around, she swung it for his head. Suddenly, every nerve in her body exploded with pain. There was no stopping her body's momentum as it lifted off the hard mat. The noise of the crowd faded and grew until stopping altogether. Big Bobby caught her suddenly slowed foot and pushed her backward. Nothing was as it should be. Lights streaked in her vision before her body was abruptly stopped by a metal pole slamming into her back. Then, darkness clouded her mind and she could only think one thing.

Boxers' Poison.

For a complete, up-to-date booklist, visit www.MichellePillow.com

THE PLAYFUL PRINCE

BY MICHELLE M. PILLOW

Lords of the Var® Series
Bestselling Shapeshifter Romance

To play...

Prince Quinn, royal Ambassador, isn't looking for a serious relationship. In fact, he's never even considered it. Hopping from lover to lover, he's content to enjoy himself, never taking anything but his work seriously. However, when Dr. Tori Elliot is sent to the palace to test for biological weapons, he can't seem to stay away from her.

Or not to play...

Tori Elliot has just finished her last assignment and is on her way to a much needed vacation. But when the Human Intelligence Agency stops her ship and demands she heads up a team on some remote planet, she knows it in her best interest not to refuse. Ever serious, she knows she's there to do a job and no matter what, she's going to act like a professional.

Meeting Prince Quinn, his body pressed against another woman in the palace halls, she knows he's not the man for her. Too bad he's the Ambassador and too sexy for his own good. Fighting her desire, Tori must try to do her job while not succumbing to the playful Var prince.

The Playful Prince Excerpt

His sudden movement caught her attention and she realized he stepped toward her. He lifted his hand, as if to touch her. Tori flinched and took a step back.

"Sir," Tori stammered. "I mean, my ... ah?"

"Quinn," he supplied with a rakish smile.

"Yes, my Quinn... wait, no." She took another step back as he moved aggressively forward. The look on his face made her heart flutter in excitement.

"Your Quinn?" he mused in a low tone that sent chills over her spine. "You wish for me to be your Quinn?"

"Stop!" she demanded holding out her hand. He paused in his quest to get to her and grinned, waiting. Tori swallowed, nervous and distracted. "Prince Quinn. I am Dr. Elliot with ESC ... well, actually the HIA, well, not really, technically with HIA or ESC except—"

Was she babbling? Tori was pretty sure it sounded like she was babbling. Scientists didn't babble. It wasn't appropriate. Her scowl deepened. Oh, why was he continuing to look at her like that?

"Well, Dr. Elliot not technically with the HIA or ESC," Quinn said, lowering his jaw as he leaned forward. "I'm H O R N Y and you're extremely pretty."

"H O...? Oh! Really!" Tori gasped, dismayed. She shook her head in disapproval.

"What? You're really so surprised? Can you really blame me, Dr. Elliot? You were staring quite intently at—" Quinn began to motion down, acting as of their conversation was an everyday topic.

Tori held up her hand and shook her head frantically to stop him. Taking a deep breath, she centered her thoughts and made a silent promise to never drink the night before a big assignment again. Surely that is why her heart was pounding so hard and why her limbs were shaking. Swallowing, she forced her voice to rigid calmness. "Is there someone I could talk to about gaining permission to search the cave systems that the biological weapons were discovered in? The HIA has requested that I clear the cave and surrounding area of any and all contamination threats."

Someone other than you, she thought, not caring if he saw her distaste for his lewdness.

Quinn's smile faded and to her surprise, he turned serious. "You think something else is up there?"

"I'm honestly not sure. The recovered weapon appears to be intact and contains enough chemical to wipe out at least five planets. From that bit of information, I would assume there was only the one, unless the caves were being used as a storage unit of some kind, which, given the political climate of your Kingdom, doesn't seem to be the assumption. From what I understand, your father was fighting a war with…"

Tori stopped, realizing that she might be speaking too candidly. That's why she hated being in political situations. Facts were facts and she was use to stating them, regardless of their popularity. In her job facts were all that mattered. In politics, a person was supposed to say things diplomatically, twisting the words into just the right phrase. It was a skill she lacked. She looked up at the Prince. His face hadn't changed. She swallowed nervously. He motioned his hand slightly for her to continue, not looking at all offended by her words.

Weakly, Tori said, "My checking would simply be a wise safety precaution for everyone concerned, especially your people. It won't cost you a thing, if that's your concern. HIA is taking care of my and the other scientists' salary."

Quinn nodded, a motion she hoped was agreement.

"My team has nearly gotten through with the palace inhabitants and so far everyone has tested negative. I believe they're about finished." Tori looked at her clipboard and pretended to scan through the data. This man unnerved her. She couldn't concentrate on what she was saying to him. Was she repeating herself? Was he even listening? Did she tell him yet that they were about done testing the palace inhabitants? She thought it, but did she say it? Damn, he had the most brilliant blue eyes she'd ever seen in her life. Delicately clearing her throat, she said, "But, we'd still like to do a thorough scan of the caves. There is no point in us leaving anything behind."

Quinn seemed to contemplate her words. Tori lowered her voice and stepped closer. He didn't move, except for those blue eyes. They followed her, keeping fixed on her face.

Getting excited, Tori forgot her nervousness as she admitted in a secretive whisper, "There was also something else. I took the liberty of analyzing the strange dark mud on the biological weapon's crate. I believe it's from your marshes, because I found some fresh moss that leads me to believe it wasn't already on the crate when it was brought here. Anyway, there was an extremely high level of what appears to be DTH12 compound, which I'm sure isn't indigenous to this particular planet, being as your swamp soil is classified as GR13H and not TDH14. What doesn't make sense is that DTH12 is primarily found in the slime trail of northeastern yellow slugs on the planet of Fluk in the H ... what? Are you laughing at me?"

Quinn was indeed chuckling. Shaking his head, he said, "Woman, I have no idea what you just said."

Tori frowned. She should have known. Sarcastically, she drawled, "Your mud is neat and I'd like to look at it."

Okay, maybe that was a tad too condescending. Quinn grimaced but didn't appear overly offended. Lucky for her, because he might just be the man she had to impress.

For a complete, up-to-date booklist, visit www.MichellePillow.com

PLEASE LEAVE A REVIEW

THANK YOU FOR READING!

Please take a moment to share your thoughts by reviewing this book.

Be sure to check out Michelle's other titles at www.michellepillow.com